DRAGON SKIN I

Bibliografische Information der Deutschen Nationalbibliothek:
Die Deutsche Nationalbibliothek verzeichnet diese Publikation in der
Deutschen Nationalbibliografie. Detailierte bibliografische Daten sind im
Internet über
Dnb.dnb.de abrufbar.

TWENTYSIX- Der Self-Publishing Verlag
Eine Kooperation zwischen der Verlagsgruppe Random House und BoD-
Book on Demand

Wir danken www.pixabay.com für die kostenlose Überlassung des
Coverfotos

Herstellung und Verlag
BoD- Books on Demand Norderstedt

ISBN 9783740751357

DRAGON SKIN I

The Members of a Dragon Family
Search for Their
Gem Stones

By Angela Paulsen

Translated from German into English
by Peggy Muench

.

.

Prolog

"My earliest childhood memory is my beautiful Mum. Her slender body had a striking light-orange coloration only disrupted by grey rhombs on her back running from her neck to the tip of her tail. She had kind maroon eyes which seemed almost lost in her triangular shaped head. The protective plates on her head also shimmered light-orange. At her jaw the dark-orange merged into grey and black. The color grew more intense the further it advanced to her dangerous three rows of spikes. When Mum was in danger or when she felt miserable, she could cock these spikes as well as her beard. It made her head look twice its original size. It was massive! Mum was able to devour an entire springbok in one go. Well, to be honest most of the time she ate plants or fruits but sometimes she also fancied meat. Our diet consisted mostly of protein as we still had to grow. That was the reason why our mother had been gone hunting so often. During those times we had to stay inside our cave and our Aunt Bernadette was taking care of us. Mum took off with few powerful strokes. Her mighty wings started above her forelegs and stretched all the way along her belly to her hind legs. Underneath her wings piercing spikes, looking like daggers, separated her upper belly from her lower belly. We kids didn't have to be careful to get hurt, while we were fooling around, since she was able to put her spikes back. Enemies were less fortunate though. They had to fight against this means of defense. We watched our Mum longingly, when she circled above our den, before she was leaving to go hunting. Her tail was as long as her body which she gracefully lashed through the air. That was the moment when I felt really proud of my family.

We are dragons, fire-spitting, springbok-devouring dragons. I was so proud of my family and so impatient.

At that time, I was neither able to spit fire nor to fly. We already had tiny bones but they wouldn't become wings before puberty, let alone placing springboks into my mouth.

To become as beautiful as my mum that was most important for me. Her beauty lies in her color that is why her name is Stella. Her body shines bright orange just like the sunset.

We all have names referring to different gemstones. That is what Aunt Bernadette had told me. We are predetermined to find our gem which will complete our body, our mind and our soul. Its characteristics supplement ours and therefore strengthen us. Our most important task is to look for this gemstone and to find it during our childhood. You might now mention that my mother's name is not a name of a gemstone. That is true. But there is a stone called citrine. It represents the power of the life-giving sun due to its shade range from lemon-yellow to orange. Additionally, it supports individualism and self-confidence. And Mum had found her citrine, which wasn't yellow but orange on a remote island. She had almost lost her life by doing so."

DRACO

Draco stretched out happily in the warm sun. This platform, perched high up on the cliff, was his favorite place. Right underneath his snout the precipice dropped down to staggering 500 dragon-lengths in depth. When he closed his eyes, he could hear the sound of crashing waves. The height of the white crests informed him about the approaching weather. Even though, it seemed as if he was relaxing, he felt rather restless. The next hurricane was long overdue. And his claws were full of tingling sensation. He longed to perform his favorite activity, which was apart from eating and lazing around,
cyclone riding!
His eye, which was turned away from the ocean, was closed while the other one was observing the water. Even before he could see the hurricane he was able to smell it. The air wetted his nostrils. Thus, he opened the other eye and slowly raised himself. The golden-black horizon revealed what he so desperately wanted to see. A hurricane was finally approaching. Very soon he would tuck his wings firmly against

his body. The wind would twist him upwards like a rocket. At the very top he would penetrate through the icy cold right into the eye of the hurricane where he would dive straight down into the depth. He would be able to do two or three of those rides. Then he would be so exhausted and hungry that he would have to look for a quiet cliff where he could relax before he felt refreshed enough to go hunting.

Real soon now! He sensed the crescendo of the waves, the intensification of the white crests. Yes, the air smelled like salt and fish. And then he finally saw it. A giant cyclone was darting at him. That would be great fun!

But what was that?! That couldn't be true! Another dragon tried to fight, with opened wings, against the powerful storm. That wasn't possible! The dragon would be smashed within seconds. Draco didn't hesitate. He threw himself from his cliff and plunged straight down at a tearing pace towards the other dragon who had already lost its consciousness. The air rushed past his body. With his last strength he grasped the other dragon and pressed its wings with all of his might against his own body. He used the hurricane's force which spiraled him counterclockwise upwards again. Never before had he noticed the bitter cold and the physical strain in such an extent. With his front claws he firmly clutched the other dragon's limp body against his own.

"Hopefully it hasn't died yet."

When he reached the eye of the hurricane he dashed down and then out of the storm. He needed a flat dry spot in order to examine the powerless body. Due to his tremendous efforts his gem shimmered in every shade of emerald. This provided him with additional strength so that he could get them onto dry land. He could neither hear nor feel the dragon's breath. Oh yes, there at the flank was a weak up and down. Thank God! But what was most surprising, it was a dragon-girl!

An attractive dragon-girl had been blown into his life.

He observed her more closely.

She was very young. Probably on her way looking for her gem. She had already got her dent from the Oracle. It was clearly to be seen on her forehead. But the gem wasn't there yet.

It was about time that he got her something to eat if he wanted her to regain her strength. Then she would be able to continue her search to find her gem. He, Draco, would help her.

STELLA

Stella saw herself detached from her own body drifting into the void of space.
"Where am I? What has happened? Am I dead?"
Her memory was blurred. The only thing she could remember was flying to the south east in order to find the Oracle. Her sister, Bernadette, had described her the way. These instructions had been handing down from one dragon generation to the next.
Her sister had also given her a rhyme which she was supposed to follow

In the east
wakens the sun and the beast
In the north
the sun leaves its brightest swarth
In the west
the sun and the beast will rest
In the south
you find only darkness and drouth

Stella had to look for a red rock called Adama's Territory which was the center of a vast wasteland. The Oracle which was also called Adama, would give her further information where to find her gem. She enjoyed flying under the warming sun. She felt light as a feather and independent.

"What will the Oracle tell me? And above all how will it look like?"

She silently glided above the dense jungle. Then she rose higher until she broke through the clouds. These looked as if they were made of cotton-wool. They constantly changed their shape and their formation. Some of them piled up to tall sculptures. She was convinced she would have been able to walk on them. Lowering her altitude again she crossed first a fjord then wasteland. A few buffalos were startled by her sudden shadow hovering across the ground. There was no reason for them to be afraid as Stella wasn't hungry.

She had already travelled for several sunrises when her eye was suddenly caught by a shape in the distance. It looked like a lost egg of a tremendous bird. Stella headed for it then perched on its summit. It was completely flat as it was exposed to wind and weather.

"But where is the Oracle?"

"I am here, Stella."

Stella turned around. A gigantic dragon, with golden scales and a diamond, had appeared out of nowhere.

"You don't have to be afraid. My name is Adama, the Invincible. I am the Oracle. And I am going to explain you the way to your gemstone."

"Good evening Adama," Stella's heart pounded wildly.

"Listen very carefully, Stella and then you will be able to find your protective stone.

In the east
wakens the sun and the beast
In the south
the sun leaves its brightest drouth
In the west
the sun and the beast will rest
In the north
you find only the darkest swarth.

Your gem shines like the sun, it'll provide you with pure energy and it'll boost your self-confidence and your love of adventure. You still have to look for food on dry land since your way will lead you across the ocean far to the north west. Use all your senses. Feel and listen to your body. It will be able to guide you. Pay attention to the wind and to the white horses. On the Island of Breaker you will find your gem."

Adama detached a scale from her chest with her golden claws.

"Close your eyes, Stella."

The Oracle pressed the tip of the scale between Stella's eyes. Stella felt a tingling sensation.

"Your body is prepared to take up your gem."

The air shimmered and Adama had disappeared.

Stella summarized what she had heard. Firstly, she had to eat, then she had to fly across the ocean to the north west in order to find the Island of Breaker.

She took off. The buffalos and springboks were less fortunate this time. When Stella had enough to eat she turned towards the north and set off. It took her a few sunrises until she reached the ocean. She had never seen such a huge area covered only by water. Although she had been brought up on Raiffa's Finger, a peninsula where her mother lived. She raised her wings and started her journey across the sea. Stella had been on her way for quite some time and more and more often she thought that her strengths were about to leave her.

When this happened, she raised herself up above the clouds where she glided effortlessly on top of an air stream.

"But when will I finally arrive? My body doesn't tell me anything."

Stella pierced through the clouds again. And all she saw was water, water, water.

"Is this never going to end?"

Suddenly she felt a tremendous blast of wind. When Stella looked down onto the water surface, she noticed that the white crests had become higher and denser.

"What did the Oracle say? I am supposed to pay attention to the wind and the white horses. Yes, but how?"

Panic-stricken she looked backwards. She saw a raging tornado arising behind her without realizing the danger. The hurricane was approaching at an incredible speed. The fierce winds shook her whole body. The noise was unbearable and scared her to death. When it caught her, she tried to escape with all her strength. But it was in vain. That was the moment when she passed out.

When Stella regained consciousness, she found herself lying on solid ground. A shiny green dragon man was looking at her anxiously. His belly was a light turquoise merging into dark turquoise which ended at his long piercing belly-spikes. Back and belly were separated by a lush green that bended into emerald green. His eyes were also emerald. But they could change its color according to his mood.

"Are you ok?" He asked. His voice was like a tolling of a great bell.

"I am Draco. That was rather foolish of you to fly into the tornado."

"But I didn't do that on purpose. I was just swept away."

That's what Draco had already assumed. Many had already lost their lives while crossing the ocean. Lack of knowledge carelessness and inflated self-esteem were often the cause. He would make sure that she ??? Yes, what was her name by the way? That she would arrive safe and sound at her destination.

"I am Draco. And what's your name?"

"My name is Stella. And I am starving."

"Well, then you stay here Stella. You take a rest while I am getting us something nice to eat."

Before Stella was able to respond he had already taken off.

She looked after him for a brief moment and then fell into a restful sleep.

Draco returned shortly after she had woken up. He held a silvery limp thing in his mouth which he put right in front of Stella.
"Try it."
"What is it?" she looked highly skeptical.
"That's fish. Don't tell me you have never seen a fish before?"
"No, I haven't."
Draco tore a bit out of the fish.
"Try it, it is really delicious."
He gave her a chunk of which Stella bit off a small piece. She chewed it very slowly.
"It's not too bad."
"See!" Draco's face broke into a broad grin.
Then they devoured the fish hungrily until nothing was left.
"What are you up to now?" Draco looked at her expectantly.
"I will set off again to find my gem. The Oracle told me to search for it on the Island of Breaker."
"I know the Island of Breaker! It is only a few sunrises away. It is a small island with a rugged coastline. You barely see its cliffs when the tide is high. The waves, coming from the ocean, break right here. Therefore, the name. Inside these cliffs there are a few caves. At high tide they are

completely filled with water. But at low tide you can get inside. I have already explored a few of them. But I have never found a gem."

"What is high tide? What is low tide? You are talking in riddles."

"I've forgotten you were brought up on dry land and not yet been to the sea. Tide is the rise and fall of the sea. It happens twice a sunrise caused by the attraction of the Warming, the White Moon and Muraco itself."

Stella glanced at him completely puzzled.

"I can tell, I have to come with you."

"Do you think that is allowed?" Stella gaped in astonishment.

"Sure. Why not?"

They started their journey flying to the north east, the shining green and the glittering orange dragon.

Stella and Draco reached the island at low tide. It was surrounded by steep cliffs. Some of them were taller than others, some were jagged others flat. At low tide it was possible to see the rocks covered with seaweeds and shells. They perched on the beach in the south of the island.

"I think, first we should have a look around. As I said, I've never seen any gemstones here. But maybe it is different this time as we specifically search for them. Maybe we should go different ways. Would you like to turn to the left or to the right?"

"I'll turn right," decided Stella.

After walking on the beach for quite some time she noticed a cave which had been hollowed by the water. It led deep inside the cliff. She went a long way down. Driven by curiosity she advanced even further and didn't notice the rising water. And it rose blazing fast. Her back was already covered by the water when she suddenly got caught up in the maelstrom.

"Not again!" Stella thought frantically.

"This time I won't black out!"

She pressed her wings very tightly against her body and closed her nostrils. With her first and second lids she had just covered her eyes when she got carried away by the torrent. She had almost run out of breath when the torrent weakened. She was able to lift her head out of the water. Still snorting she had a look around. She was swimming in a black lake. Above her she saw a dome shining in a bright lemon-yellow. At a closer look she noticed that it was covered with countless gemstones.

"I've found my gems!"

Now it was time to find the right one for her. She examined the rock face and the ground with a searching gaze. Suddenly she saw it. In the middle of the wall was the perfect gem for her. Lemon-yellow right size perfect for her drop-shaped dent. Stella flew right up there to scratch it out with her claws.

"That obviously doesn't work."

Stella thought for a moment, then she made up her mind. She would try to detach it by shooting a jet of fire at it. It was a rather difficult task as she had to spit fire just in the right intensity and at the same time, she mustn't drop the gem. Finally, she was successful. She held her protective stone in her claw! Due to the heat of the fire it wasn't lemon-yellow anymore but shimmered in all possible ways of orange. Stella placed it into the dent on her head. She felt a tingling sensation running through her body.

"I've found my gem! Now I am grown-up. But how will I get out of here again?"

Stella considered various possibilities. Should she try to find the same way back? How long would that take? Maybe the torrent would return. While pondering she was staring at her feet.

"My feet. I can see my feet."

The tide was slowly falling and it revealed several underwater passages. She headed towards the brightest one even though the water level was still a bit higher up here. She would need some patience.

"How much time has gone by? Draco will definitely be worried by now."

Stella followed the winding path. Behind the next curve it led upwards. At this point the water had already completely disappeared. At the next bend she was able to look into a deep crater and from above the sun shined brightly.

"Hooray!"

Stella jumped into the crater and spiraled herself up into the air. She didn't stop until she had reached the upper outmost edge of the crater. She was right in the middle of the island surrounded by the blue brilliance of the sea.

"And again, the ocean. It is about time to find Draco and to finally get home."

She returned to the spot where they had parted. She found Draco pacing restlessly up and down the beach.

"Stella where have you been? I've been looking for you all over the place."

After looking at her more attentively he gasped,

"Sincere thanks to Adama, you have found your gem!"

"And you are so beautiful!" he thought to himself.

"Yes, and now it is time to settle down."

"But before you do that, I will show you our wonderful world."

Draco's favorite cliff was their first destination. They spent a few sunrises there. Draco showed her how to interpret the waves according to the wind, how to fish and to enjoy the prey. Later on, they skimmed across the southern part of the island before they reached an estuary which they traversed. Finally, they arrived at the shore of a huge continent called the Northern Continent. An impenetrable rain forest stretched to the north as well as to the south. They perched on a sandy bank by the sea. Draco caught some fish to which Stella had gotten used to by now. Then they continued their journey. They moved to the west. The scenery varied from humid and tropical jungles to wasteland and arid deserts.

"Well, I really should be on my way to find my new habitat,"
Stella became restless. Draco, who had always preferred to be on his own, didn't want to admit that he felt so happy and content as if after molting. He didn't want to let her go at all. When they both looked at each other, Draco's emerald changed its color from its usual dark green to turquoise. Then it gleamed like the lagoon where he had been born. Stella's gem blazed in any orange shade.
"I just want to show you the Assembly Place. After that we will look together for your new home. And then I'll leave you alone."
They had been traveling about thirty sunsets when Draco pointed downwards.
"We are about to arrive at the Assembly Place."
The Green Canopy had thinned out. The savanna extended in all directions surrounded by mountains in the far distance. This was the place where The Great Gathering took place. Every 200 rotations all dragons came together for this event. Every dragon was delighted to meet relatives, acquaintances and friends, most of whom hadn't seen each other for

a very long time. Draco had chosen this place to perform his dragon-dance. He was nodding his head and circling around Stella when he cocked his beard.

"What will she do? Will she cock her beard as well? Will she nod her head? Or will she raise her right claw to signal her agreement?" he pondered.

They were facing one another. Draco raised his head and cocked his beard for the last time. Stella lifted her right claw in order to indicate her submission. After this mating ritual the copulation could begin. They stayed two more sunrises in the clearing. When they were leaving the place, Stella noticed another dragon circling in the far distance above the mountains. It alighted on a cliff which looked like a dragon's head.

"Do dragons live in this area?"

"Not that I know of."

They didn't pay any further attention to it. Draco still wanted to show Stella the Ten Thousand Islands of the Rising Sun located in the western ocean. But Stella became more and more impatient. She finally wanted to find a home of her own. Therefore, they took off flying to the south.

On their way they decided to visit Stella's mother, Raiffa.

But after that Stella finally wanted to find the place where she could settle down.

They reached the peninsula called Raiffa's Finger shortly before sunset.

Bernadette, her sister, was lying next to the cave.

"Hello Bernie, what are you doing at Mum's? I thought you had found yourself a home a long time ago. By the way this is Draco. He has saved my life. And he has also helped me to find my gem."

Her enthusiasm deterred her from noticing her sister's reserved behavior. Then her mother emerged from the mouth of her den. She was a turquoise and sand-colored dragon with a jagged coral on her forehead. Everything about her was tubby. A tubby head with friendly tubby eyes. Tubby cheeks arched over her spikes so, these were barely to see. She had a tubby belly and tubby thighs. She needed her tail as a counterbalance, so she wouldn't tilt forwards. Her wings, however, seemed rather small. Due to her body structure flying caused her great difficulties. She tried avoiding it whenever possible. But she was a kind-hearted dragon. She treaded everybody with the same motherly love and care. Whether they liked it or not.

"Hello Mum. This is Draco. We are looking for a home for me. We won't stay for too long."

Bernadette signaled Stella that she wanted to talk to her alone for just a short moment.

"How dare you bring a dragon man to Mum's cave?" she asked sharply. "And even worse; you want to show him your home where you are going to live with your hatchlings? I can tell, you are about to lay eggs."

"Bernie, this will be the father of my hatchlings. Are you crazy?"

"In any case I am going to come with you. And I am going to look after you and your young."

"Although, I don't think that this is necessary I am looking forward to living with you in the future," Stella acknowledged softly.

Draco stood apart from the three ladies. He only had eyes for Stella.

"You know what I don't understand? Your mother lives on a peninsula surrounded by water and she has difficulties flying. Why has she never been hunting in the ocean?"

"Well, she mentioned once that she had had a traumatic experience in the ocean a long time ago when she was still young and slim. Since that day nobody has ever been able to get her back into the water. In the beginning she claimed that she couldn't dive properly. That is the reason why she taught us to go hunting by ourselves at a rather early stage. Bernadette and I are land animals and we eat what we can find on dryland."

After a few sunrises all three of them left Stella's mother. They were on their way to find a home for Stella and her hatchlings. Time pressed. Her flanks were already bulged due to the eggs. There were six of them. They headed towards the south-east and crossed the Hakan Desert. After some time of straying they reached a prairie at the northern edge of the Uplands.

"I think this is perfect. All we have to do is to find a suitable den."

That wasn't a problem for them. They found a hollow which led far into a mountain. The soil inside was nice and sandy. The peaks nearby had flat ledges and dead trees were scattered everywhere. This would be a wonderful adventure playground for the young. They had found Stella's new home. But parting from Draco made Stella rather sad.

"We will see each other very soon, my dear. As soon as the young have hatched, I will come and visit you."

Bernadette looked at him suspiciously but didn't say anything.

It didn't take long and Stella started to dig a hole inside the den. She examined the consistence of the sand, verified the temperature and the humidity. She closed the hole again and dug another one where she then deposited her eggs. She buried these, neatly arranged, in the sand. Exhausted, she lay down next to them. From now on she would watch over these eggs day and night with only very few interruptions. Bernadette, her caring sister, brought her food and looked after her. Stella seldom left the cave or went hunting. During these rare times Bernadette guarded the eggs, as both of them were afraid of enemies. And then the miracle happened. A tiny dragonhead appeared peering curiously out of the egg.

"Bernadette, you are an aunt!"

Little by little six hatchlings emerged from their eggs. All of them had a big triangular head with the wide eyes, a slim body and four skinny legs. What were supposed to become dragon-claws one day, still looked like feet with five long toes. Their thin tails were almost three times as long as their bodies. These were the only characteristics which they had in common. Sandy, sand-colored with remarkable blue eyes was the first who emerged from her egg.

Followed by Rubi, maroon colored with brown eyes.

Nero, the black fur bundle with an orange belly was the next.

Rocket, with his grey close-banded scales was rather inconspicuous. He emerged from his egg a bit later.

Sparkle, the exact opposite of Nero, had white short fur and blue eyes. He was the last but one to hatch.

Silent Wings took her time. She didn't follow her siblings until the next sunrise.

Time went on. The wild little hatchlings grew up. Stella and Bernadette were busy keeping them under control and feeding them. In the beginning the two sisters had to go hunting for all of them and get their food into the cave. Every one had their own particular needs and wishes. But when Stella saw her off-spring sitting next to each other or behind one another on a mountain ledge overlooking the scenery, she felt very proud. This was the best time for Bernie and herself. The most relaxing time for them, on the other hand, was right before sunset when the hatchlings wanted to listen to a dragon story. One of their favorite stories was about Berhane and Erwaen.

Huddled together in the cave, all six of the young hatchlings waited expectantly to hear Aunt Bernie's story about their ancestors, ears eagerly pricked. Only Nero kept his distance from the others as he often did. But he was still close enough to hear the story.

"Aunt Bernie how long does it take you? We are waiting for you,"

Sparkle could hardly wait.

"I am coming."

Bernadette made herself comfortable next to the hatchlings and started to tell the story.

"This old tale was handed down to us by our mother. Our mother had heard the story from her mother, our great grandmother, and so on.

Many hundred thousand rotations ago the dragons lived very peacefully next to each other in a remote world. But then one sunrise, two powerful dragon men got into a quarrel about a specific territory. The problem got even worse because of a beautiful dragon lady that lived in this very territory."

"Are you saying that two dragon men got into a quarrel because of a female dragon?"

Rocket just couldn't hold back his outrage. Bernadette giggled to herself,

"Yes Rocket, that can happen, even here."

A murmur of amusement rose and then quickly ebbed away again, as everybody wanted to hear how the story would continue.

"Well, in any case this quarrel got out of control and in the end, every dragon family was affected all over that world. It was a really brutal war. The most powerful dragons robbed the gemstones of the weak dragons. And that gave them even more power. The weak ones died miserably. Our ancestors Berhane, known as The Shining Light and Erwaen known as The Wise, were so disappointed in their fellows of their nation that they decided to leave that world and to find another place to live. They were able to hover through space and to find shortcuts between the different universes. Finally, they alighted on this planet. The Shining Light and The Wise are the ancestors of each and every one of us in this world that live on mainland. Our gemstones had been brought to this planet by them. Originally these gems had belonged to their former world. Due to the radioactive radiation from space, the stones' efficiency and intensity had been both significantly reinforced. The first and only daughter was Adama, the Oracle. Her unique character is due to the fact that her egg was already in her mother's womb when her parents were travelling through the galaxies. Her characteristic features had been influenced by the uncountable and various radiations.

"Wow, she must be pretty old," remarked Nero, puzzled.

"Yes. And she will become even older," explained Bernadette.

"And you have to know that only once every 100 000 rotations a dragon hatches that is able to fly through space. And water-dragons hatch only once every ten thousand rotations."

The siblings got very excited about all this. That hadn't been Bernadette's intention at all.

"How can you tell that one is a water-dragon?"

"Am I a water-dragon? I'm already webbed,"
Nero stared at his webs in astonishment. Bernadette was struggling to answer all these questions. To stop the discussion, she promised to continue the story at the next sunset.

But when the offspring dashed in different directions which often was the case, Stella and Bernadette had a hard time. The young were always chasing after something that had moved even if it was only a sibling's tail. Their thin legs carried them blazing fast. The two grown-ups had their difficulties keeping them under control.

The girls played being mothers. They dug holes, measured temperature and humidity, buried eggs and kept an eye on them. They looked for small egg-shaped stones which they would put in the prepared holes. Then they turned around, having their backs to the eggs, and with their forelegs they covered these with sand. With their rear legs they shoveled the hole up completely. The clutch of eggs was watched very carefully by them.

The boys' games were harder and rougher. They pretended to look for gems, to fight imaginary foes, to defeat the enemy by turning the opponent onto its back and to discover the whole continent which meant to explore the surroundings.

From early on Stella noticed some hostilities between Sandy and Silent Wings. Especially Sandy always demanded to have the things their sibling were just playing with. She also always wanted to be the most beautiful one. Stella tried not to pay too much attention to it.

The little dragons were on fire when Stella and Bernadette announced that it was time for them to learn how to fly. One morning they took their young to practice take-off and landing. Unfortunately Rocket had to walk with Bernadette as he still hadn't learned how to lift his body into the air.

They looked for a cliff which offered an ideal runway for every dragon. This was a rather difficult task as every one of them had a different approach how to take off. Their approaches were as diversified as their appearance and their character. Stella showed them how to run downhill, to unfold their wings, and how to drift leisurely through the air.

Sandy wanted to be the first one as usual. She started to run, flapped her little wings but then dropped down. Again, she tried flapping her wings and again she sank further toward the ground. She repeated it a dozen times. The landing was also problematic. She landed heavily. With her four legs and her snout, she dashed onto the ground.

Rubi lunged forward and with a few powerful strokes of her wings she was in the sky, climbing rapidly. But landing caused her some problems too.

Silent Wings was the born glider. She raised herself into the air, strained her wings and soared up. She used every little air draft. After circling effortlessly a few times she perched gracefully. Sandy's anger was boundless. She wanted to hover as elegantly as Silly.

Rocket on the other hand, didn't know at all, what to do with his wings. He had watched Stella how she had been running down the hill. When it was his turn, he did it just the way she had done it before. While running he tried to spread his wings. But he

33

wasn't successful. He took his run-up over and over again but each time he ended up with his snout in the dirt.

"It's just not possible that I cannot fly. I am a dragon!"

"Some need more time others less. You have to have patience," said Bernadette softly.

Rocket grumbled to himself and watched his siblings from the distance.

Nero took two, three steps, unfolded his wings and took off. While landing he touched the ground first with his rear legs and then with his forelegs. Just as it should be done.

Watching Sparkle, one could barely imagine that he would be able to fly at all. True, this roundish fur bundle had everything one needed in order to fly; broad wings and a long tail to navigate. However, he looked far too round. With his body structure he couldn't possibly get off the ground. He stamped a few times with his front legs before he started to run. It was a rather mediocre performance. The landing on the other hand he passed with flying colors.

They all practiced a few more times.

Stella enjoyed watching her young when being with them up in the air. They started to take advantage of the updraft and even began to chase each other playfully.

At the end of the day they were fooling around. They hurtled through the air, headed towards each other then veered quickly away from collision before surging back into the sky again.

Neither landing nor take-off was a problem anymore. After everybody had alighted Stella instructed them to fly home. Everybody did except Rocket. He had no other choice as to walk back with Bernadette.

But this was still a huge progress as all of them were able to go hunting from then on. Stella had chosen an ideal hunting territory for them. She killed their prey and divided it up between the off-spring right then and there. Only Rocket's food she had to bring back into the den. But she was confident that he would join them very soon too. The time would come that he would also be able go hunting by himself.

NERO

While his brothers and sisters were playing outside Nero was lying alone in a corner of the cave. He didn't want to join them. He was bored. And the bright sunshine made him squint his eyes. He had a strong aversion against sunlight which heated up his short black fur. The heat was unbearable for him. He rather buried himself halfway in the damp sand and stayed inside of the den.

Why was he the only one in the family who had this disposition? A black furry back and an orange colored belly which could be seen ten dragon- lengths against the wind. His already strong claws were webbed. The talons were of orange color too and razor sharp. It wasn't surprising that his siblings complained to their mother when he hurt them accidentally or when he teased them because he felt so miserable. He was bored to death.

The food his mother brought him he didn't like and he didn't know what to do with all his strength.

But when they were flying to Lake Emerald he was in high spirits. At the southernmost end of the lake was a spectacular waterfall that plunged down into the depths of the lake. It was a marvelous playground. Several caves were hidden behind the waterfall. He loved to discover these together with Sparkle. Playfully they dived in and out of the frosty water and explored the cool refreshing hollows. That was fantastic!

As his other siblings preferred to stay on the shore it was no fun to play with them here either. They just dipped their claws into the cold water for a short moment. But when they came to these disgusting lukewarm ponds, which had formed next to the lake, they could spend hours splashing happily in there.

"Yuck! How revolting."

Sparkle was the only exception since his short dense white fur was water-repellent. He didn't like fresh water though. He was constantly coughing and spitting water when he went diving with his brother. But they had figured out one thing: When they were playing hide and seek or when they were chasing each other underneath the water surface, they were able to communicate with one another,

"Hello Nero, where are you?"

Nero was able to understand these words and when he answered him,

"I am here. Keep looking,"

then it wouldn't take long and Sparkle had found him. Only the maximum distance to communicate, they hadn't figured out yet. Nero loved the fresh water of the lake whereas Sparkle preferred salt water. Therefore, they didn't play together in the lake as much as Nero would have liked it.

He felt very lonely. Nobody really understood him. The worst moment for him was shortly before sleeping when the others snuggled up. They were laughing and giggling until they fell asleep. Nero would have loved to join them. But it was far too warm for him. He listened to every noise which made him wide awake again and very angry. Angry about himself and the way he was.

ROCKET

"Mum, Mum have a look! Look, what I can do!"
Rocket raced excitedly up and down, whirled around and then stopped abruptly in front of Stella. He had cocked his beard and spread his wings. Now he quickly folded these tightly which made his silver-colored scales clung even tighter to his skin and made them hard as steel. With his mouth wide open, not fire, but a semicircular translucent ball appeared and built itself up around his triangular head. This way his head got hermetically sealed. Even though his head was airtight now he was still able to breathe. His body automatically performed some sort of a recycling process which enabled him to keep breathing.
Nothing astonished Stella any longer. The genetic variety of her offspring had only been a surprise for her during the first few days after they had hatched.
Rocket kept experiencing his body's capabilities over and over again. He was able to take off vertically. He just had to unfold his wings. Inside these a recoil

system helped him to build up the necessary energy. When he reached the desired altitude, he pressed his wings against his body which made his titanium scales rock-hard and the helmet built itself up around his head. Then he was able to dart himself into the atmosphere. Each time a bit higher and a bit further.

As it would still take some time, before he'd be old enough to start looking for his gem, he would use that time to practice flying higher and further. Until now there was no end in sight. And his gemstone would even reinforce these extraordinary abilities many times over as soon as he'd possess it.

He was fascinated by the view onto his habitat from above. When he raised himself into the air, he was able to see a huge landmass surrounded by water in the east as well as in the west. When he soared even higher into the sky, he had a gorgeous view of his illuminated planet. It looked like a blue ball dotted with white clouds in the black of space. Maybe he could show all this to his family one day. He pushed himself to the limit but at this time he couldn't rise any higher. On his way back, he realized that the ball around his head served as a protective shield. The

friction, when entering the atmosphere, generated a tremendous heat. It was much more intense than any dragon fire.
"One day I'll be ready to go to the Oracle," he thought to himself.
"I have time."

SANDY

Sandy had turned into a pretty dragon lady. She was just as beautiful as her mother. Where her mother was shiny orange Sandy was creme-white and fawn-colored. Unfortunately, her beauty only referred to her appearance and not to her character. She felt envious, was conceited and resentful. Her family members just shook their heads at her tantrums. Sandy didn't even try to hide her negative attitude, let alone trying to get rid of it. She pretended to have so much self-confidence that the others thought she was arrogant, whereas in fact she was just very shy and uncertain. In order to compensate her insecurities, she started to pilfer dragon-skin powder from an early stage on. Her mother made the powder out of molted skin. The best effect she achieved when taking a mixture of Rubi and Aunt Bernadette's skin. After the consumption of this powder she felt creative, powerful and superior to her siblings. And exactly this was the main reason for her dishonesty. Neither Silent

Wings nor any other brothers and sisters should be better or more beautiful than her. "I just have to be very careful not to take too much of Aunt Bernie's skin otherwise they might notice it. Rubi's skin shouldn't be a problem as she is growing so fast. She molts at regular intervals."

One day a bright green dragon was

circling above the den.

"Kids, your father is coming!"
Stella announced excitedly, her heart filled with joy.
"Bernadette, have a look! Draco is visiting us!"
"If only he visited." Bernadette muttered grimly.
She gathered the kids around her. Together they waited for Draco to land.
"Hello everybody! Stella, what an adorable bunch of kids!"
Stella stood proudly in front of her young.
"Kids, this is your daddy Draco!"
It was as if a signal had been given, everyone raced towards him, started speaking at the same time and crawled up onto him.

"Daddy, are you staying with us from now on?"

"Are we going to be as strong as you are one day?"

"Where did you find your gem? It is huge! Was it dangerous to get it?"

Draco endured it all calm and patiently.

"You are already so big. You and your wings have already grown so tall and strong. How are your flying skills?"

The little dragons looked sheepishly away.

"Well, then we want to practice it during the next days. As soon as you can fly properly you will be able to start looking for your gem. But before that we are going to attend The Great Gathering. There you can watch the Council of the Seven Stones punishing offenses and administering justice. There is a lot to see. You will be astonished."

"What is the Council of the Seven Stones?" asked Nero his father curiously.

"The Council consists of seven adult dragons. They come from the different habitats of Muraco, The World of The White Moon. These Favored Few are supposed to represent their own specific interests at the Council. The Oracle determines the intermediary between The Wise and itself.

Their protective stones are supposed to be the most powerful ones. No gem may appear twice. Unfortunately, we are only six dragons right now in the Council of the Seven. The appointment of the seventh member takes the Oracle a long time."

"Why, we?" Rocket asked his father with a grin.

"Because I am also a member of the Council. The Oracle has to appoint the seventh gemstone. Our seven gems have to be combined before we have our complete power capability."

Bernadette watched Draco suspiciously. Even though, he was a member of the Council of the Seven Stones Bernadette felt rather uncomfortable. How could the hatchlings trust him so easily?

GREAT GATHERING

"Do you really want to go to The Great Gathering?"
Bernadette looked at her sister anxiously.
"But of course. The kids are already very excited about it. And so am I. Besides, Draco will be there. We are going to look for a resting place which is a bit off the main area. This way it will be easier to keep an eye on the kids. You should also have some company."
Stella winked at her sister mischievously.
"You should get to know a vigorous dragon."
Bernadette tried to evade the subject.
"But not now. I stay here with the kids and you fly and enjoy The Great Gathering."
"That is out of the question. You are just looking for an excuse not to join us. The kids cannot be stopped any longer. We are leaving."
"You have six kids. And we are only two who will look after them. You know very well, that the gem-robbers stop at nothing. They are friendly and nice to the little dragons and then they'll steal their protective stones. In the end you'll find only

their corpses, if you are lucky. But the corpses will be maimed and the stones will be wrested. Do you really want to risk that?" Stella meekly pointed out that also Draco would come to the Gathering.

"Dragon-men,"

explained Bernadette harshly,

"they have only one thing in mind when attending The Great Gathering. Their own pleasure while playing and mating. I cannot imagine that your Draco is an exception to the rule."

The kids as well as Stella kept trying to convince their good-natured aunt Bernadette to agree and to join them on their way to The Great Gathering.

It only took place every 200 rotations. Every little dragon waited eagerly to attend their first Gathering.

But Bernadette completely disagreed. She tried to talk Stella and her offspring out of their plans. She used her own means.

Her chance came when the kids wanted to hear another goodnight story. She chose the following one,

"I am going to tell you the story about the most terrible Gathering that has ever taken place.

It happened many, many sunrises ago. Everything was as usual. Entertaining games and dances, barter deals, meeting relatives and acquaintances. Nothing out of the ordinary. Just the oppressive humidity which had already been up in the air since that very morning seemed menacing. In the afternoon a sudden thunderstorm rolled in. The sky turned dark grey almost black. Before wind and rain were able to take the edge off two bolts of lightning crackled through the sky. One right after the other. Immediately followed by two ear-splitting thunderclaps. The dragons were absolutely terrified. None of them had ever experienced anything like that before. A sudden turmoil on a small plateau, where the young had stayed, drew the dragons' attention. Every mother darted immediately to the plateau. One little dragon was lying motionlessly on the ground. His playmates reported that he had been on the highest peak when his tail shot up in the air. His entire body had been surrounded by a white light. Since then he hadn't moved. The mother of the little dragon knew straight away what had happened. She gathered his friends and their mothers so that they could say their last goodbye. Then she led them away and selected some dragon-men who watched the little body and made sure that no one would come to this dangerous place until the electric tension had completely vanished. As soon as the place was safe again the little dragon was transported directly to the Assembly Place where they burnt his corpse. This was possible as he hadn't found his protective stone by then. Very sad songs were sung during the ceremony. The Great Gathering got terminated by mutual consent directly afterwards. Nobody was in the mood anymore to celebrate, since a little dragon had just lost its life."

"Why didn't the little dragons look for shelter after they had seen the lightning?" Sparkle turned uncomprehendingly to Bernadette.

"You know, Sparkle, sometimes the forces of nature are so fast that we don't have a chance to react quickly enough."

The young started chattering anxiously all at the same time.

"You always have to pay attention to the signs of nature when you are looking for your gems. Will you promise that?"

"Yes, Aunt Bernadette!"

The kids chorused.
At this point Stella became really furious.
"Bernie, you can do whatever you like but we are flying."

Many things had to be prepared.
Package-leaves were collected and adjusted to each dragon. They were used to carry the beloved fruits which were just about ripe to be picked from the trees. These would be fermented by the time they would arrive at the Assembly Place. They were valuable means of barter. Especially dragon-men preferred these fruits. Sometimes it became rather embarrassing to watch them after they had eaten these fruits. Their usual proud and upright walk turned into a stagger, the look of their eyes into a blank stare and their words into a babbling without rhyme or reason. It had already happened that an uncontrolled jet of fire caused immense damage. But for Stella and Bernadette these fruits were easily obtainable objects for bartering. This way they wouldn't have to go hunting. Especially during the time of The Great Gathering there would be very little prey since so many dragons would be hunting in the same area at the same time.

Without the necessity to go hunting they would be able to look after the young and enjoy the festival.

Even more valuable would be the kids' skin. As long as the young dragons were still growing, they shed regularly. Their skin always met strong demand by the healers who also attended The Great Gathering. Stella had to ground the skin immediately after the shedding. If she waited too long it would turn stale and unusable. Each skin had a different effect. It varied according to the dragon's skills and features. Stella's mother had already taught her daughter a lot about dragon-skin powder. Stella's skin was used by the healers in order to purify the patient's soul. Bernie's ground skin was recommended to boost creativity. Ruby's powder was very precious. It had a revitalizing effect and was used as a strong remedy. As Stella hadn't been able to figure out the effect of Sandy's skin, she would ask the healers how it could be used and how much it would be worth. Neither was she able to analyze Nero's skin. It appeared to be rather spiritual which was a complete contrast to Nero's body that had shed it. Rocket's powder on the other hand would serve many dragons as a verity-powder. With the help of Silent Wings' skin, it was possible to distinguish between friend and foe as well as between good and evil. The effect of Sparkle's skin astonished her. Her furred pet was able to deliver a powder which could enhance virility.

At the Gathering the healers had a wide variety of different skins from various dragons which they mixed to compose many different blends.

Stella would hide half of it in their cave at home. The other half she would take with her and offer it for trade. Each of the dragon-kids was allowed to take one personal item. Then finally the time had come to set off. Their journey would last about thirty sunrises. On their way they wanted to break the journey and visit Stella and Bernadette's mother so that she could meet her grandchildren.

After an exhausting flight they arrived on grandmother's peninsula. The young were overwhelmed by their grandmother's massive corpulence.

Sparkle whispered to Nero,

"Look, Nero. Even her knees are tubby."

"What do you mean, my dear?" Raiffa asked softly.

Stella threw them a deprecating glance.

They stayed a few sunrises at Raiffa's before they took off again, bright eyed and bushy tailed.

The kids got impatient. It couldn't be fast enough.

"When will we arrive? How long does it take?"

The number of dragons in the air increased the closer they got to the Assembly Place. They all had the same destination.

"Kids, have a look, down there is the Gathering,"

Bernadette pointed at a clearing which was packed with dragons.

"We are going to look for a resting place aloof from the crowd."

Stella headed towards a spot which she had already agreed with Draco to use.

"Sincere thanks to Adama!" No one had discovered it yet.

It was a bit off the Assembly Place, located in a small clearing with an opening at the front. The jungle stretched all the way up to the clearing and behind the clearing lay a huge rock that provided some protection.

As soon as they had stowed away all their belongings and had arranged their sleeping places, the kids instantaneously wanted to head to the Assembly Place.
"We should wait until your daddy is here. We cannot leave our shelter unattended. You have to have a bit more patience."

It didn't take long when an imposing green shining dragon appeared above the clearing.
Sandy pointed upwards,
"Daddy is coming!"
After the excitement about his arrival had settled, he received one of the valuable fruits out of their storage. And then Stella Bernadette and the young set off for the Assembly Place.

All eight of them strolled through the traders' lane. They bargained here and tried there. Nero and Sparkle caught sight of a dealer who traded in dried fish. Attracted by the marvelous smell they desperately wanted to try a bit of the delicacy.
"Mum, what's that? Can we taste it? Mum, please! It smells absolutely fantastic!"

Sparkle also approached and savored the smell.

Their siblings just wrinkled their nostrils and tried to get away from the stench.

"Please Mum, only a bite."

Stella agreed and exchanged a few pieces of dried fish against some of her fruits.

Nero and Sparkle devoured the pieces right then and there.

"That is so tasty! Why can't we have that more often?"

Stella looked at Bernadette and remarked, "As father, as son."

None of them noticed the dark-pink greasy dragon with his dull rose quartz. The gem didn't fit properly, hadn't been nicely adjusted and looked shadowed.

This dragon followed them wherever they went with an evil grin.

"The boss will be delighted. Six dragon kids accompanied by two dragon-ladies. And neither of these six has got their protective stones yet. If that doesn't look promising. One or two of these precious objects should be easily obtainable."

Stella, Bernadette and the kids left the traders' lane and crossed the clearing where other dragon families had set up their resting places. The boys were especially interested in the men's meeting points where these consumed the popular fruits. Another favorite attraction was the dragon-dance. The participants danced until exhaustion. The noise level was approaching the pain threshold. Dragons laughed, blared, discussed and argued heatedly with one another.

Rocket was completely mesmerized by the dragon-dances. The opponents circled around each other, cocked their beards and changed their colors according to their mood. The gems on their foreheads sparkled brightly when they tilted their heads backwards before they tossed them forward again. A music band beat the dragon-skin-drums. The spectators stamped their claws on the ground to the rhythm of the music. One song Nero learned immediately by heart:

Adama, Adama
the colorful dragons
come to you
prepared to fight

Adama

They come from far away
to get their mark
Adama

The holy rock
visible from far
leads them to you
Adama

Adama, Adama
If good, or bad
you help us all
to find our stone
Adama

Nero would have stayed the entire sunrise with the fire-shooters. They competed in a long-distance fire-shooting tournament. Rubi was interested in the booths of the healers. These wise women blended dragon-skin-powder according to ancient formulas in order to produce medicine, stimulants, tranquilizer, love potions and other remedies. Sparkle was fascinated by the young wrestlers. These had just previously found their gemstones. He also wanted to take part in these competitions as soon as he had found his own gem. The physical diversity of the different dragons intrigued the kids greatly. Some grown-up dragons had no wings. Others had wings, but their bodies shimmered in all colors of the rainbow. Also, some of the protective stones blazed in the most dazzling of colors. Stella informed her young that they would also meet their other grand-mother, Draco's mother, during these sunrises.

After some time of strolling around, marvelling, and chatting here and there, they finally returned tired but happy to their resting place. Draco was already waiting for them impatiently. He also wanted to attend and enjoy the Gathering but in his own way, in a masculine way.

Bernadette, Stella and the kids were just standing at a trader's booth who sold or exchanged fruits, when suddenly a turmoil spread across the place. Customers flinched, traders retreated hastily behind their goods, so Stella and Bernadette were now able to see the cause of the turmoil. A flame-red dragon strode down the lane surrounded by his fellows. His eyelids were only slightly opened. He examined his surrounding haughtily.

Bernie immediately acted. She harshly ordered the kids to stay behind her.

Stella didn't understand Bernie's behavior. The red dragon approached, was then taken aback for a moment and came closer them. He sneered,

"Hello Bernadette! You look amazing. How are you?"

Bernadette turned ice cold and stiffened. This was the dragon she had once trusted completely and who had betrayed her unscrupulously.

"Now I am fine! And one day you are going to pay dearly for your evil deeds."

Charc burst into raucous laughter which roared across the clearing.

"Well, I am curious how you want to make that happen. Let's go, guys!"

With one of his claws he gave her a poke on her chin while little whiffs of smoke rose from his nostrils. Bernadette hated these whiffs. She had already detested them in former times since it was a sign that he was sexually aroused. In the past she had put up with it.

"Take your filthy claws off me!"

She snorted at him angrily.

"Otherwise I am going to burn a mark into your forehead."

Uncertain how to respond, he glared at her then moved on with his run-down companions releasing a steady stream of curses.

Stella stared at Bernadette in great astonishment.

"Bernie, who was that? What do you have to do with him?!"

"That was Charc, The Red. This is the dragon who broke my heart. He kidnapped and murdered my three kids. The first three stones in the lower rays of his five-point star, are the ones which once belonged to our children."

"Why have you never told me? I am your sister!"

"Stella, I just couldn't. It was far too cruel for me. But one day I will tell you everything."

CHARC

Charc's companions were delighted as he was in very good spirits. The encounter with Bernadette had uplifted his mood. Even though she had tried to hide the young, without gems; he had noticed them all.
And...
He had already chosen his favorite one. This little white fur-creature would definitely get an interesting stone.
Charc's skin as well as his claws were blazing red. His black pupils stood out against his fire-red eyes. In comparison with the other dragons he had not only one gem, which was a black diamond in the shape of a five-point star, but in addition he also had various small jewels on each prong of the stone. These were the bloodstones which he had taken from his kids who had to die for that.
He tried to obtain more and more stones in order to become more and more powerful. One day he would be the most powerful and the strongest dragon in the world.
He had already sent out his pink companions to look for potential victims.

"It would be lovely to get two additional dragon-kids. That would make this Gathering a real success."

"Folks, the next is on me. I'll treat you. Life is wonderful!"

THE COUNCIL OF THE SEVEN STONES

Draco had promised to take his young to the Council of the Seven Stones. He had chosen a petty crime as he didn't want to scare the kids when the jury delivered its verdict.

"Stella, you should join them."

Bernadette tried to convince her sister to accompany Draco and their offspring.

"No, I am not going. And you are staying here, too. The kids can go to the Council without us, just with their father."

Gloomily Bernadette confirmed,

"Just as you like."

"Give me one reasonable explanation why the kids shouldn't go with their father. Nothing is going to happen to them."

"It's ok. Let it go at that."

Hence, the little sons and daughters went with their father, Draco, to the Assembly Place.

The council members were sitting in a semicircle. Two places hadn't been taken yet. Draco informed his young where they should stay and took one of the empty places for himself.

"The seventh member still has to be selected by the Oracle."

Sparkle shared his knowledge eagerly with his siblings.

"Look at him. He represents the interests of the oceans."

Nero pointed at Hinto.

"He looks rather peculiar."

Despite the fact that the continental mainland of Muraco, the world of the dragon, only comes up to less than twenty per cent, the underwater world of this planet was almost unknown. Hinto's appearance regularly astonished even the representatives who were sent to the Council of the Seven. He had a silver-grey body covered by close-banded scales. In the middle of his dragon-head rested an extraordinary white pearl. His teeth were remarkable. He had many rows of sharp teeth which wouldn't allow his prey to escape. He barely didn't have any talons. But between these, webs were to be seen. His gills were right underneath his ear-openings. He was able to close the gills and to inhale oxygen instead whenever he was on dry land. He breathed through a little opening above his ears. His wings were huge. He wasn't able to fold them firmly. So, they hung limply next to his body when being on dry land. That made him look a bit clumsy. But as soon as he was inside the water this sight changed completely. Elegantly and weightlessly he glided through his ancestral element. He used his tail as a propeller when he needed to speed up.

"But look at him, he looks great!"

The representative of the jungles, Adahy, looked totally different. He was as colorful and noisy as his habitat. On both sides of his mouth light green stripes stretched along up to his ears, merging into a light blue. The bottom side of his mouth was an exact mirror image. Only a little spot of orange was to be seen at his nostrils. A black line shaped like a S, separated his head from his body. His underbelly was lemon-colored. Just around his black eyes the light blue marking appeared again. The rest of his body was covered by black feathers. His protective stone, an agate, shed colors ranging from lemon-yellow, to light-green and light-blue.

"And that one, Silly, he looks just like you!"

Rubi pointed at Chockop. He had been sent to the Council as the representative of the air. He had a light-blue silky plumage ranging into white at the wingtips. His protective stone was a noble sapphire. Rocket looked around and remarked, "But our daddy doesn't look bad either." His siblings murmured their agreement. "And that one over there is probably the representative of the deserts." Rubi meant Hakana, who seemed to be a self-confident dragon. "She is absolutely gorgeous," she muttered. The delegate of the deserts shimmered in a soft beige. But if one took a closer look sparkling grains of sand glinted in all pastel colors. Her gem, a calcite, glowed orange. "And look, that one, who looks like Sparkle, he is definitely in charge of the ice deserts." Nero was talking of Yas. "If I find my habitat in his area then I won't have to sweat any longer," he answered quick-witted. Draco glanced at his kids disapprovingly. Immediately they stopped their conversation. A run-down pink dragon was led in. He was accused of destroying the belongings of a dragon-family with his fire, after having enjoyed too many of the fermented fruits.

The council decided that he should work for that very family until he had made up for the damage. Hakana detached a scale from her chest before she attached it to the convict's. From now on she would be able to follow him everywhere should he try to cheat justice.

This was an exciting event for the kids. Babbling all the way along they followed Draco to their resting place.

"And now? Has anything happened?" Stella asked Bernadette.

Bernadette turned away without a word.

Despite the unpleasant incident in the trader's lane Draco Stella Bernadette and the kids enjoyed happy sunrises. Shortly before flying back home Nero came running to his mother panting for air and heart painding, he yelled,

"Mum, Mum! Sparkle is gone!"

"What do you mean by gone?"

"We wanted to get some of the delicious fish and therefore went to the Trader's Place and then we wanted to watch the performance of the vagabonds but he had suddenly disappeared."

"Bernie, Bernie!"

Stella hurried to Bernadette.

„Stay with the kids. I am looking for Draco. We will search Sparkle together."

It dawned on Bernadette immediately.

Stella spreed her mighty wings and took off to find Draco or even Sparkle from above. It didn't take long and she was able to make Draco out. In the middle of a crowd of male dragons he was showing off his muscles.

She noticed at once that he had already consumed quite a few of the fruits. But when she told him what had happened, he was immediately sober. Together they scanned the entire Assembly Place. They asked everybody whether they had seen a little dragon who looked like Sparkle. They found out that two more dragon-girls had gone missing. Until now Draco hadn't really been concerned. He had been convinced that a little dragon had lost his way on the Assembly Place but would return home safe and sound in the evening. But three little dragons gone at the same time and gem-robbers on their way. That did worry him indeed.

"Stella, I'll rush to the Council of the Seven. Then I will gather my friends. We will search the area. You fly to Bernadette. Get your things together and ready for your departure. You have to head home."

While Draco set off to find his friends, Stella returned to their resting place. Bernadette was already waiting impatiently, fearing the worst.

"Have you found him? Please Stella, tell me that you have found him!"

She whimpered in fright.

"No, Bernie. But I think it is about time now that you told me your story. We have to know everything about this red dragon."

Bernadette hesitated.

Stella's voice became quiet and menacing.

"Bernie. This is about one of my kids. I need to know what had happened."

And Bernadette started to tell her devastating story.

"I have always tried not to awaken painful memories. But you are right, you have to know,"

she admitted meekly,

"I had just found my gem and rested exhausted but happy and very content at the shore of the northern ocean. Adama had shown me this area. It hadn't been difficult for me to find my gemstone. There were thousands of them lying on the sandy beach. The only challenge was to find the appropriate one for me. But even that wasn't difficult. It was just lying there in the sand. A remarkable transparent oval was blazing in the most dazzling of colors ranging from beige and orange to light brown. When I took a closer look, I noticed a heart-shaped fawn-colored pearl in the center of the stone. And when I tried putting it in the dent, which Adama had provided me with, it fitted perfectly. I sensed at once the soothing effect the stone had on me.

I was just about to take off to look for my new habitat when a bright red dragon appeared behind the dunes. I pondered shortly whether to fly away or to stay. And then decided to stay. If only I had flown far away; as far as possible.

It was Charc, The Red. We talked with each other and we started to like each other. At that time, he wasn't as ruthless and evil as he is nowadays. I just realized that he was much weaker than I was whenever we played and fooled around with each other or when we went hunting. He became raving mad when he got aware of it. I didn't mind pretending that he was much stronger than I was. I restrained myself and thus we had a wonderful time together.

Maybe I shouldn't have done that. If I hadn't behaved like that, it probably wouldn't have happened.

I got pregnant. It was about time to find myself a home. He accompanied me and therefore knew where I would stay. Then he flew away.

I was such an idiot. All he wanted to know was how he could easily find me and my hatchlings.

Well, the eyes of love are blind. Otherwise I might have noticed that he had always concealed the truth from me about his origin and his habitat.

When I had asked him about his habitat, he just smiled and said,

"In order to find me you had to fly to the other end of the world where sand and water boils. It is just a place for a cool guy like me."

A little later my three kids hatched. They were so adorable.

When they were old enough to fly it didn't take long and Charc came to visit us. I thought he was the loving father, who is delighted to see his offspring. Well, he was delighted but from a different perspective than I had assumed.

We enjoyed a wonderful time. And when I had to go hunting he offered to look after the kids. I thought nothing of it. When I returned and none of the four were to be seen I still didn't become suspicious. But after the sun had set three times and still nobody had returned I started to panic. Where were they? What has happened to them? What could I do?

First, I started to search the immediate surroundings. Nothing. I was completely helpless. They could have been everywhere. Then I decided to fly to the Oracle.

"The one you loved betrayed you.
The most precious he took from you."

My kids? Where are my kids? I begged desperately for an answer.

"The spirit of two of your kids is detached from their body
The soul of the third one is going to follow soon
Their gems are lost

Until the sinner will have received its fair
punishment
mourn their passing
They will keep living in your heart
In due time
hand the gems over to the blazing fire
which is born from the ocean."

The only thing I had really understood was
that two of my children were dead. But
dragons live thousands of rotations. What
had happened? And where could I find
their bodies?
I decided to head home in order to make
further decisions there.
The first shock was already waiting for me
when I arrived. In front of the cave I found
my firstborn lying in fetal curl as if it was
sleeping. But she didn't sleep. I bent down
to my daughter and shook her body. She
had to wake up! But she did not. She was
dead. When I kneeled next to her, I
noticed that she had already received her
dent by the Oracle and that she even had
possessed her gem. But it had been
violently burned out of the kid's head."
"That is horrible,"
said Stella, shuddering.

"Who was able to commit such a cruel crime? Had it really been Charc?"

"I asked myself the same question. Or was I suspecting the wrong one? Well, I ran into the den where the next shock was waiting for me. Archie and Chally were also rolled up just like their sister. But what was that?! Archie wasn't dead. A weak up and down at his flank showed me that he was still alive. I hurried towards him and tried to lift his head carefully.

"Archie, what has happened?"

Weakly he whispered,

"Mum, Dad has hurt us."

These were Archie's last words.

Now I knew. Charc was the one who had killed my children.

On this day my heart got captured by iron claws. Since that day I feel completely numb. Neither happiness nor grief can touch me. I still grieve for my kids. Without them it's hardly worth living. I hate Charc for what he tore from me.

I also put Lapis, my daughter, into the cave and then I shot fire at it until the rocks collapsed and I hadn't a single spark left in my mouth. When I collapsed from exhaustion, I saw that the rock had turned into a huge diamond which enclosed my kids.

I stayed with my beloved ones for a few rotations during which I mourned freely, and then I returned to our mother. The rest of the story you know."

"What a horrible loss for you. But why did he kill his own kids?"

Stella asked her sister with unspeakable grief in her eyes.

"That is very easy to explain. He isn't as strong as he would like to be. He wants to enhance his own power and which each stone, he can steal, his strength grows. The first stones he stole, were the ones which were most easily to obtain; the ones of his own young.

And now you also know why I treat all male dragons with great suspicion. A second Charc could be on its way. Please give Draco my sincere apologies. It has nothing to do with him personally. But what the kids is concerned I really blame myself. We just haven't been careful enough."

In a way, Bernadette felt relieved that she had finally shared her story. No longer would she be alone with her terrible secret.

CHARC

Charc and his dragon-fellows had looked for a secret retreat before The Great Gathering began. It was so far away from the Assembly Place that no one would have assumed to find any dragons there. But for those who knew the place, it was easy to find. It was a cave located underneath a rock which looked like a dragon's head.

After Charc had also kidnapped the other two dragon-girls, they just waited for the sun to set in order to fly directly to their hiding place. They were heading eastwards. It took them a few sunrises before they reached the coast where Charc and his companions went different ways. The older dragon-girl had to accompany Charc immediately to the Oracle. Sparkle and Diane, that was the name of the younger dragon-girl, had to fly with the Pink Brigade to their hiding place. They moved up from the south. After a few sunrises they turned towards the east again.

"I know this area,"

whispered Diane to Sparkle.

"The place where I grew up isn't far from here. And we often went on long excursions."

Sparkle replied,

"I am convinced that our parents are looking for us. We just have to leave them a signal at each resting place and whenever we change direction. But what could we use as a signal?"

Diane and Sparkle thought frantically while surveying the area. But no idea came up. The search party would be flying. Where and how could the dragon-kids have left a signal for them?

They crossed large and small islands which were surrounded by estuaries. After another change of course towards the south Diane remarked,

„That is Chendris, the Green Continent."

For a few sunrises they moved along the coast until they reached the southernmost part of this continent; the hiding place of Charc and his Pink Brigade. It was located in the middle of the jungle. Trees blocked the place from view.

The Pink Brigade were a lazy bunch of dragons. Diane and Sparkle had to hunt their own food. Of course, they were constantly under observation wherever they went. But they weren't able to prevent Sparkle from contacting his brother Nero.

"Nero, can you hear me? Nero, please can you hear me?"

He didn't receive an answer. But he kept trying.

After a few sunrises Charc appeared in the secret retreat. A new gem adorned his forehead. A deafening cheer went up from his fellows. To the delight of his companions he had brought enough ripe fruits to revel seven sunrises in a row.

In the meantime, he examined his captives over and over again. One could see how he was thinking. It made Sparkle and Diane sick when they noticed his glance. As soon as Charc was sober again he addressed them,

"Well, I think it is about time that you got your gems! In order to save some time, we will fly together to the Oracle. We will decide there who will get their gem first."

He could barely hide his craving.

"You go, catch your fish one more time and then we will set off."

Desperately Sparkle plunged into the depths of the ocean.

"Nero, Nero can you hear me? Please, pretty please Nero, you have to hear me!"
"Sparkle, Sparkle, is it you? Where are you?"
"We are on Chendris. But where exactly I don't know. This dragon, Charc, has kidnapped us. Diane and I are still here with his companions but he wants to fly with us to the Oracle to find our gemstones. He had kidnapped three dragons at The Great Gathering. Besides me there were two dragon-girls. With one of them he had already flown away. When he returned she wasn't there anymore. But he had a new stone on his forehead."
"Oh, Adama! I am trying to reach daddy. We will fly to the Oracle. Be brave! We will help you."
But Nero didn't hear an answer.
"You were supposed to hunt fish not to splash around in the lukewarm water."
Charc angrily scolded his captive. "Hurry up!"
The Red, his two victims and two of his companions flapped away across the ocean in the direction of Adama's Territory.

Bernadette and the kids had only just arrived at their cave when Nero began to get restless.

"Aunt Bernie, it is time. I have to set off to find my gem."

With a sorrowful sigh Bernie answered,

"I know. Very shortly it will be about time for all of you. I've just hoped that your mother and Sparkle would have been back before you leave."

Bernadette gave him rough directions how to get to the Oracle. He broke his journey briefly at Lake Emerald to catch fresh fish before he took off again towards the east. He traversed mountain ranges with green hills, jagged cliffs and snow-capped peaks. They ran from the north to the south where they bordered a vast savannah. He also had to cross this area before heading towards the next stage of his journey which would be a huge peninsula, Adama's Territory. His mother as well as his aunt had given him this information. And right here in the middle of the prairie he found Adama, on its rock which looked like a bird's egg. Adama, shining like gold, had the most impressive diamond on its forehead. The Oracle gave him the following instructions:

"Far you have to fly
towards the north-east
across The Huge Water

You will find the Ten Thousand Islands of
the Rising Sun
and here
dark as the night
it will constantly radiate light towards you
Not where the water seethes and hisses
neither where hot lava flows
A peaceful island in the middle of the
roaring sea
is the mother of your gem
Hidden in flesh and lime
in the middle of a salt water lake
waiting for you to commit a small blunder
in order to put an end to your life"

"Well, that sounds great!"
Hhe thought sarcastically while touching
the dent that Adama had left on his
forehead.
"A hole! A circular hole! How could a
gemstone fit into that?!"
How would that look like on his forehead?
And again, Nero felt betrayed by his
destiny. Even though he wasn't really
interested in searching this stupid thing, he
set out on his journey. He was flying steadily
towards northeast for many sunrises. When
he became hungry he swooped down on
its prey to catch some fish. Fresh fish. They

weren't as delicious as the dried fish he had got from the trader at The Great Gathering. During the course of his flight he attained a certain routine. He learned how to avoid fierce storms as he had figured out how to detect high winds due to the sizes of the tossing waves ahead of time. This enabled him to avoid the evil danger. After many, many sunrises the first island appeared on the horizon, a small island with a beach blazing in all colors. A few palm trees in the middle of the island were the only vegetation.

"I have to have a closer look; a beach full of gems."

When he alighted on the colorful pebbles they splintered into thousands of tiny pieces.

"What's that? I 've never seen anything like that before."

But as his protective stone couldn't be on this beach, he didn't stay any longer but resumed his journey.

"Are these really ten thousand islands? Or is it only the name? I will be grey and light-orange by the time I have found this round whatsit."

Nero kept flying. The islands became more numerous. And then suddenly the grey ocean seethed beneath him. A fountain spouted out of the water. Ash and rocks erupted.

"Well, that's not it."

Despite that, he felt confident to be on the right way. The next island lay mysterious and unexplored, only made up of black wasteland. Orange glowing lava poured out of a few openings. It slowly flowed down the mountains into the ocean where it disappeared with a hissing sound. Nero realized that his own colors were similar to the colors of the island. But he knew, he wouldn't find this whatsit here either.

After hovering aimlessly above the roaring ocean, he suddenly noticed a peaceful island in the middle of the sea. In the center was a crater of an extinct volcano covered by dark green jungle. In the depth of it lay a shining black lake. Nero alighted on the lip of the crater.

"What a joy! I've never swum in black water before!"

He was determined to check first, if it really was salt water. If not, he wouldn't dive into the dirty brew. He would rather look for a lake that was more appealing to him. But it was salt water. Lava had shaped a passageway underneath the earth thousands of rotations ago before it emptied into the ocean. The sea-level rise had flooded the passage and had formed a salt water lake.

Nero concluded,

"I have to descend into the intense darkness of this lake in order to find my stone."

He had decided to slowly discover the lake. He wanted to make the necessary inquiries while staying on the edge of the crater and then slowly expand these; further and deeper. Unfortunately, that didn't work as the crater was too steep. Nero had to dive in; deeper and deeper each time. His eyes adapted gradually to the conditions. He started to enjoy himself. He was able to switch automatically from above-water to an under-water mode. He was also able to stay a little bit longer under water each time he dived in. Strange looking creatures crossed his way. During one of his dive sessions, when he was only a few meters above the bottom of the lake, he noticed a snake-like fish passing a peculiar formation. It looked like a huge egg which had been opened in its middle. The cut was wave-shaped and the second halve of the egg fitted perfectly into these waves

so that it could be tightly sealed. The fish nibbled at the edge of this formation. Before Nero knew it, the two parts snapped up and half of the fish was gone. The two halves didn't open until the fish had completely been digested by the shell. "Unbelievable!"
Nero remembered the Oracle saying:

"Hidden in flesh and lime
in the middle of a salt water lake
waiting for you to commit a small blunder
in order to put an end to your life"

He definitely didn't want that to happen. He needed a strategy. How could he keep the halves stay open so that he could search inside for – whatever it was - without losing a claw, a part of his tail or even his head. Suddenly he had the idea. He needed a suction tube, which was strong enough to withstand the murderous power of these two parts. It had to be strong enough to hold them apart from each other. The correct placement of the tube would be absolutely crucial for him so that he could suck the object of his desire out of the shell. He swam back up to the surface to find a suitable tool. According to his theory he had to find a tube which he couldn't bite through either, but burn off with his jet of fire. He skimmed across the neighboring islands. A tropical island aroused his interest. After he had perched on the shore, he inspected the interior of the island. Fallen trees and drooping lianas that wasn't what he had been looking for. But there a fallen, hollow tree caught his attention. He would shorten it according to his needs. And with its help he would try to outwit the shell. With his powerful claws he grabbed the hollow tree trunk and plunged with it into the black depths of the water. He placed the log in the middle of the shell. The two halves snapped together immediately but without breaking the wood. Now it was Nero's task to suck the flesh out of the shell. He sucked and sucked, but to no avail. Nothing moved; on the contrary, he had the impression as if he had heard a noise of breaking wood. He had no other choice. With one of his talons he carefully reached through the trunk and inside the shell, trying to touch the bottom of the shell. His razor-sharp claws could feel the flesh in which a solid ball was embedded.

"Round! This whatsit is round!"

With an almighty tug he pulled at the muscle until he finally sensed that the fibers slowly loosened. But at the same time, he also noticed that the wood started to yield. A final massive jolt and he could withdraw his talon.

"That was close!" he sighed in relief.

Both parts of the shell snapped together with a tremendous force. His leg and his claw were still inside the log. But the part of the tree was,

"Sincere thanks to Adama",

outside of the shell. He surfaced again, his leg still inside the trunk and the mussel flesh with the ball inside his claw.

First of all, he freed himself from the trunk and then inspected his treasure, a ball shining in the most beautiful silverish black. That was his protective stone, a perfect black pearl. He inserted his jewel in the dent on his forehead. When he felt a tingling sensation running through his body, he knew this was what he needed to possess to be a mature dragon, fully and completely.

With an unknown peace and inner balance Nero decided to look for his new habitat. He knew his inner voice would tell him the way. But before taking off he wanted to discover the island. He had already been curious, when arriving, how and where the seawater had been able to enter the crater. When he had been diving, he had constantly sensed a maelstrom. Sometimes it had pulled him towards the open sea other times in the opposite direction. Before anything else, he wanted to discover the reason for that. Therefore, he dived to the bottom of the salt water lake once again and waited for the maelstrom to set in. He had floated for a while when he finally noticed the drift. It gently intensified and then pooled its forces in an underwater passage which streamed steadily downwards. He swam and swam. Nero had to press his wings tightly against his body so that he wouldn't get hurt. The water pulled at him more and more strongly. Suddenly he could penetrate the gloom and caught a glimpse of a glimmer in the distance. Using his last strengths, he closed his nostrils and hurtled up towards the light. He looked around in surprise. He felt all at sea because he was a considerable distance away from his island; in the middle of the open water.

"Oh man! Why do I always have to come up with such stupid ideas? Well, at least now I know this is a passageway which leads to the open sea."

Nero had found a passage which had been formed by the volcano's last eruption. The molten lava had flowed downhill underneath the earth and had hollowed out a tunnel before it drained off into the ocean. But the tunnel had remained and had continuously hardened out over the time. The rising sea-level had flooded this area and created the salt water lake.

Nero swam happily through the piercing blue water, content with himself since he had been so successful. He enjoyed the water and dived playfully into the ocean waves. All of a sudden, he heard a voice, "Nero, Nero can you hear me? Please, pretty please Nero, you have to hear me!"

"Sparkle, Sparkle, is it you? Where are you?"

"We are on Chendris. But where exactly I don't know. This dragon, Charc, has kidnapped us. Diane and I are still here with his companions but he wants to fly with us to the Oracle to find our gemstones. He had kidnapped three dragons at The Great Gathering. Besides me there were two dragon-girls. With one of them he had already flown away. When he returned she wasn't there anymore. But he had a new stone on his forehead."

"Oh, Adama! I am trying to reach daddy. We will fly to the Oracle. Be brave! We will help you. Sparkle, Sparkle!"

But Sparkle didn't answer anymore.

CHARC, SPARKLE AND DIANE

Upon arrival at the Oracle's cliff The Red decided that Diane should get her prediction first.

"For all fights prepared
it will sharpen your spirit and your mind
One of the Ten Thousand Islands conceals it
At the bottom still hot
at the top already cold
The correct timing
determines whether it will be gained or lost."

Charc savored the prediction.
"For all fights prepared."
What an incredible loot had fallen into his clutches. The Ten Thousand Islands he knew as well. This looked like a no-brainer to him.
"Now, let's see what this little fur-creature has to offer. It's your turn."
The Red pushed him forward.
Sparkle reluctantly flew to the top of the cliff. Just like Nero, he didn't want to hear

his prediction. But this was due to different reasons.

"Sparkle, I am Adama. Keep faith. This is your advice:

Noble forces by a deity
enclosed in your stone
will protect you from evil
and negative spiritual influence
Biting wind
Eternal day
Eternal night
that will be your habitat
But your gem you will find underneath the
scorching sun
twinkling through the sweltering desert
sand
shining in all colors of the rainbow."

Sparkle decided to alter the prediction a little bit so that he could gain some time.
"Well, what has the Oracle told you?"
Charc was waiting impatiently.

"Noble forces by a deity
enclosed in your stone
will protect you from evil
and negative spiritual influence
Biting wind

Eternal day
Eternal night
here you will find your gem."

He repeated very convincingly only the first part of the Oracle's prediction which he had slightly changed.

The Red grinned wickedly.

"The Oracle has been really generous to the two of you. I only know one spot in this world which corresponds to this description. It will be rather convenient to fly back to our secret retreat. And you baby, you will see The Huge Water and the Thousand Islands for the first time in your life. Let's get going! We are flying back!"

After telling The Red the wrong location Sparkle started to doubt his decision. He'd just wanted to gain some time. But returning to Charc and the Pink Brigade's hiding place wouldn't help them at all. Nobody would ever find him.

Draco and his friends had had a thorough search of the entire Assembly Place but hadn't found anything. He was crestfallen when he returned to their resting place.

"Draco?"

"Yes, Stella?"

"Can you remember showing me the Assembly Place?"

"Yes, of course."

"Can you also remember that I asked you whether any dragons live in that area?" She asked him expectantly.

"Now, as you are mentioning it, yes. Why?"

"Because I had seen a dragon alighting there on the peak which looks like a dragon-head, above the northern mountains."

She looked at him, searching for hope.

"Let's go! Let's have a closer look!"

Exhaustion and hopelessness seemingly disappeared. With new momentum both of them set off to continue their search.

They found the cave; deserted!

"Someone must have been here quite recently,"

Draco concluded as remnants were spread all over the place.

" It looks like a hasty departure."

"Stella we mustn't lose any time. We have to get to the Oracle at once."

The shortest way to Adama led via Stella's cave. By mutual consent they broke their journey there in the hope that Sparkle might had returned home in the meantime.

But their hopes got dashed again. This emotional roller coaster wore them out. First hope was growing when they thought they might have found a trace about Sparkle's whereabouts which then got destroyed again. This caused them deepest despair.

At Stella's cave they were also told that Nero had left to find his gem.

Silent Wings convinced her parents to accompany them to the Oracle, as she also wanted to head towards Adama. Stella and Draco anticipated potential danger, nevertheless, they didn't oppose their daughter's plan.

Aunt Bernadette stayed behind with Sandy, Rocket and Rubi.

But soon it would also be time for them to start looking for their protective stones.

After they had arrived at the Orcale's, Draco left Stella and Silent Wings behind in the prairie as he wanted to speak to Adama on his own. His emerald showed that he was one of the messengers between the Oracle and the Council of the Seven. But today he came with his own personal matter.

"One of my kids has been kidnapped. Can you give me a clue who the culprit is and where I can find him? "

"The same dragon who possesses
bloodstones on his forehead
The same dragon who has also
kidnapped other parents' kids
that is the one
you have to look out for
Obsidian and Opal
you have missed
The direction is the same
which they have taken
The Red will separate them
A Black Pearl will bring them back
But pay attention to resentment and
grudge
which endanger everything."

Stella and Draco were devastated when they realized that they had been too late once again.
"But Adama also said that a Black Pearl will bring them back.
Maybe things will turn out for the better."
Tentatively, Stella smiled at Draco.
"We don't give up! They are coming back!
If only I could find a possibility to support

the Black Pearl. Right now, we can't do anything but wait. The best place for you to wait is at home and I will fly further on to the Council of the Seven."

Draco and Stella said goodbye to Silent Wings and returned to Stella's den.

Due to her light-blue body, the almost translucent wings and her soundless movements in the air, one only noticed her when she had already alighted. Scarcely audible she had landed on Adama's platform. The Oracle was immediately willing to provide her as well with the desired information.

"Not far away from your place of youth
surrounded by the rolling waves
lies the Island of the Damned
clear and pure
A six-sided jewel
will adorn your forehead
But pay attention
to the inhabitants of the island
who have lost their wings a long time ago
You won't have a permanent home
but will become a wanderer
in the service of the dragons."

After receiving her mark, she spread her wings and glided through the air to find her gem. She kept flying northwards above the shore along the piercing blue sea. After several sunrises she discovered an island that was covered by a dense jungle. A tingling feeling inside her mark informed her that she was on the right way; The Island of the Damned. She had to find a stone that looked like a six-sided prism. And its colors had to resemble the colors of her body.

"This island is completely overgrown! Well, I can't clear the entire woodland just to find my gemstone."

Silly headed towards a hill which was the beginning of a mountain range which stretched from north to south. The thick forest caused her quite some problems to land. She was used to gliding and to come down on even ground. But how should she find enough space between all these trees which grew so closely to one another? While trying to land she suddenly caught sight of a clearing on the slope.

"That could work."

Silly spiraled herself back up into the air then approached the hill once again from the valley of the mountain. Flying up the hill, she just managed to alight in the clearing.

TOO EARLY

Sandy was pacing up and down the den. Rage had welled up in her. Why was Silent Wings allowed to accompany the parents and she wasn't?

"When Silly", that was Silent Wing's nickname, "can look for her gem, then I can do that too. I just have to convince Aunt Bernadette that I am able to travel the long distance and that I can find my stone."

That wasn't difficult for Sandy to do.

Before she asked her aunt for permission to start her journey she had pilfered some of the ground dragon-skin again. After swallowing it she experienced an unknown vitality running through her body. She felt invincible.

"That was great! That was absolutely terrific!"

Bernadette was a bit surprised that Sandy was so hyper. But as she was more concerned about Sparkle's disappearance, it was pretty easy for Sandy to dispel her aunt's doubts. And so, it happened that the disobedient dragon-girl followed Draco, Stella and Silent Wings.

She kept sufficient distance, waited until her father had returned from Adama and observed him and Stella flapping away. In order to avoid any risks, she decided, to stay at a safe distance until Silly had also returned from the Oracle. As soon as Silly was out of sight, it was finally her turn.

"Now, I can search my gem."

She alighted on the cliff and awaited Adama eagerly.

"Oracle, where are you? Oracle, I am here! Sandy, Stella and Draco's daughter. I came to hear my prophecy."

Nothing happened. If Sandy hadn't seen her father and Silly leaving the rock right after each other, she would have thought to be at the wrong place. Or she might have thought that the Oracle doesn't even exit. She called once more,

"Adama, I am here. Sandy. I've come to receive my guidance. I'd like to get my gem!"

A gigantic pillar of fire forced Sandy to back off.

"Here I am, Sandy, Draco and Stella's daughter."

"You came too early
Your time hasn't come yet

Clear your character
When your soul is purified
you may search your protective stone."

"That is so unfair! Some of my siblings are as old as I am. They are already on their way looking for their jewels!"

Adama didn't answer. She had vanished. Entirely baffled Sandy stayed behind on the rock. Maybe she should have taken some of that dragon-powder. Maybe that would have made her appear more mature. The Oracle would definitely not have noticed it.

"I won't head back. I will try to find my gem without the Oracle's prophecy."

She left the platform, hovered several times above the cliff and then veered to the east. She crossed the country. As soon as she reached the shore of The Huge Water she turned northeast.

"Have I demanded too much of myself?"

When traversing the ocean, she saw a few islands which offered her a place to rest. It was a long way. And this wasn't even The Huge Water yet.

"Do I really want to go to The Huge Water? I'm not sure."

After many, many sunrises Sandy noticed a faint green line on the horizon.

"At last, mainland again!"

She reached the coast in the early evening. A jungle bordered the sandy beach.

Even though, she was a dragon she was scared to death by the impenetrable forest and its strange noises. She rolled herself up as she had done when she had been a hatchling and tried to sleep. But it was completely in vain. It wasn't until dawn that she finally drifted off into a deep but fitful sleep haunted by nightmares. When she opened her eyes, she was facing three run-down pink-colored dragons. The gems they possessed were rose quartz. None of which had been edged correctly.

"Now this is an unexpected pleasure! This will reduce the trouble we are going to get in. Our boss will be less upset that this bloody fool has been able to escape, now that we can instead present him this baby who hasn't got her a gem yet."

The second added,

"I think I saw her together with the two dragon-girls and the other boys. I call that a stroke of luck."

"Well, then come with us, baby. We'll show you our home. Heh-heh!"

NERO

Nero headed right back home. On his way he kept plunging into the ocean waves as he hoped to hear Sparkle's voice again giving him an idea about his whereabouts. But he wasn't successful.

After he had completed half of his journey back to dryland, he stopped to rest on one of the little islands. When he suddenly saw two dragons on the horizon. He was just about to make himself noticeable when something held him back. The two came closer and at that moment he felt very thankful.

"Sincere thanks to Adama. That was The Red! And the other one was probably Diane. The dragon-girl Sparkle had mentioned.

What am I supposed to do? As long as Charc is on his way with Diane, Sparkle cannot be in jeopardy. Nobody knows where they are. But Diane won't be able to defend herself. I have to help her! But how? I don't have a plan."

Nero followed Charc and Diane at a safe distance. He hid himself behind bands of cloud and made sure to stay out of sight.

Gradually he noticed that their destination was obviously the place which he had just left.

"Funny coincidence," he wondered.

Charc and Diane approached the island. It consisted mainly of solidified magma. But even now hot lava was emerging out of a few openings which then flowed down the crater into the ocean. Neither seaweeds nor moss grew on this inhospitable cliff. Nero watched The Red talking harshly to Diane. Then they flew towards a nearby palm-tree island.

"What shall I do? How can I rescue her?"

Then he had an idea.

Once a sunrise an enormous cloud of ashes and rocks erupted from one of the openings. It always took place at the same time but only lasted for a very short moment. Ashes and rocks then quickly disappeared again. They diffused in the air or sank into the deep water of the ocean. Somehow, he had to distract Charc right before the outburst, get Diana's attention and escape with her in the passageway where he had found his pearl on the crater's bottom.

"No problem at all," he thought sarcastically.

"That cannot work."

He was still swimming in the sea when he saw that The Red and Diane circled above the island again. They crossed the isle a few times. Then Charc turned around whereas Diane kept discovering the area. It couldn't take that much longer before the volcano would erupt. Nero was ready to take off. It rumbled and roared. The ash cloud shot up into the sky right between Diane and Charc separating them from each other.

That was the moment for Nero to spiral himself up into the air.

"Diane, I am Nero! Sparkle's brother. Hurry up, I will rescue you."

Diane didn't hesitate for a moment. She followed Nero immediately. They dashed off briefly above the water surface.

A green island came into sight in the distance.

"Can you dive?" he asked anxiously.

"But of course."

"Wonderful. Then come with me. Press your wings very closely against your body. And keep focusing on my hindlegs. Hurry up!"

Diane did what Nero had told her. Both of them submerged; very far and very deep. Diane had never dived such a long distance before. And then everything turned pitch dark. She felt a drift which helped her to follow Nero. Suddenly the dragon changed directions. They moved upwards.

"Where are we?"

She surveyed the deep black lake, the wall of the crater and then spotted the azure blue sky above them.

"This is the place where I have found my gem. We can hide in here for some time."

"Oh Adama, I am so thankful."

Nero looked at Diane.

"You have an awesome dent."

Diane hadn't been interested in the form of her dent yet. Until now she had only worried about her life. Slowly she touched the dent on her head. It started on her forehead and carried on to her snout.

"That's an arrow."

Charc had settled down on the neighboring island. He couldn't help the little dragon. She had to find her gem by herself. But as soon as she had found it he would be right there to take it away from her. This had to be done immediately after the stone was brought to life. As that was the moment when the stone was most powerful for him. Normally the force of the gems grew along with the young dragons. But he had to take the gemstone with the amount of power it was provided with at that very moment.

He constantly kept a keen eye on Diane when he suddenly felt a rumbling underneath his claws. The lava crust broke open and a tremendous cloud of rocks and dust burst into the air.

"What was that? Where is the little one?"

He surged into the sky at once and hurtled around the island.

"Where is she? She can't just vanish into thin air."

He tore around the island a few more times. But there was no sign of Diane. He would wait until the ash cloud had settled and then he would continue his search. She had to be somewhere. She couldn't have escaped. He wouldn't let her get away.

Charc looked for her on the isle and in its vicinity for a few sunrises. Rage gripped him. Grimly he hissed,

"That is just not possible. I don't lose such a valuable jewel! This stupid dragon has to be somewhere. Did she get hurt by the ash cloud and the rocks? But in that case her body has to be somewhere on the island or it has to be drifting in the water."

He became increasingly frustrated while searching her.

"This little beast hasn't been able to fled, has she? Or did she die? If that is the case, I've wasted lots of time."

The Red alighted on the isle. He shot a jet of fire which made a lava spill look lousy. Then he soared up into the air again and left the island. He was still spitting fire while dashing to the west.

"I'll get you for this, little fur-creature. You will pay for this. The day will come when I burn your gem slowly out of your forehead."

He was blind with rage; just staring ahead of himself. Otherwise he might had noticed that his departure was attentively watched by two dark dragons which were floating in the deep water.

Sparkle mused frantically on how he could escape. He had already found out that the members of the Pink Brigade disliked water. Whenever they told him to catch his prey, they just hovered above him and observed him closely. Maybe this could be his chance. Each time when Sparkle went hunting he tried to contact Nero, but he was obviously beyond reach. He couldn't find a way to communicate with his brother. But one sunrise his biggest dream came true. Nero responded.

"Sparkle, can you hear me?"

"Nero, where are you?"

"I've found my gem. Charc and Diane crossed my way when I was searching my new habitat. I followed them. I was able to rescue Diane. How long is it ago that The Red left your hideout?"

"About thirty sunrises."

"Sparkle, you have to get out of there. He'll be back soon. And Sparkle, he is raving mad."

"Ok. What are you going to do?"

"Diane and I are going to look for her gem. And afterwards, I am absolutely sure, I'll see you at Mum's."

"As Adama wills. I will try. Nero, we keep in contact."

Sparkle caught another fish and then swam back to the shore. But next time he'd try to flee. Charc wouldn't get him. He would rather die.

Nero and Diane didn't forsake their hiding place for a few more sunrises. They wanted to be absolutely sure that The Red wouldn't

return. But then the time came that they felt safe enough to start searching Diane's gem.
"What did the Oracle tell you?"

"For all fights prepared
It will sharpen your spirit and your mind
One of the Ten Thousand Islands conceals it
At the bottom still hot
At the top already cold
The correct timing
determines whether it will be gained or lost."

"I can understand why The Red is outraged that he has lost you. I think you were already very close to your destination. I discovered an island, when looking for my own stone, which has solidified. Come on, let's check it out immediately."
Even though neither a tree nor a bush was growing on the isle Diane had a positive feeling when approaching it. They perched close to the beach.
"I'd like to seek my gem on my own, Nero. Please, would you stay here and wait for me? If I am not back after three sunrises, you can start looking for me."

"That's ok. I'll be waiting for you right here."
Nero watched her spreading her wings and flapping away.

Time passed and she didn't return. His hopes began to crumble away. But then on the third sunrise, he was just looking eastwards, when he noticed a dragon soaring through the air towards him. She was flying right in front of the rising sun. Diane was a mature dragon now, fully and completely, due to her gem. Her claws and legs were a shining dark-grey which merged into a light-grey towards her lower belly. Her massive spikes separated it from her upper belly which was a glossy black. Her back was also black. But there were colorful stripes running from her snout to the tip of her tail. Black merging into dark-turquoise, light-orange, turquoise, yellow and again turquoise. These stripes were also on the opposite side of her body just mirror-inverted. An obsidian enthroned on her forehead. The arrowhead, which pointed into the same direction as her mouth, possessed all of these colors. The shaft of the arrow was black and shiny.

"Diane, you are a warrior maid!"
Nero exclaimed admiringly.
She turned away bashfully but proud.

Nero wanted to return to his mother's cave as soon as possible in order to find out if there were any news about Sparkle. He had tried to contact him under water during the last two sunsets. But he had heard nothing.

"I am so curious to hear how and where you've found your stone. But I think we'll have plenty of time to talk about it while flying home. You are coming with me to my Mum's, aren't you?"

"Oh yes, of course I am."

For Sparkle very soon the opportunity was at hand to escape. To the delight of his companions one of the Pinks had brought many overripe fruits. They could barely wait to savor them. As they assumed that Sparkle couldn't spit fire yet they used lianas to tie his four legs to a dragon-tree. Then they started to enjoy their feast. Sparkle noticed that, with the increasing amount of consumed fruits, they started to lose control of themselves. They laughed raucously and the atmosphere got boisterous. They told the wildest stories which became more incomprehensible with each fruit they had devoured. It took an endless time, as it seemed to Sparkle, until the first one fell asleep. Gradually the others sank also into sleep. Noisy snoring sounds came from the clearing and small clouds of smoke trailed from their nostrils into the air.

"Now or never."

Sparkle started pulling at his bonds. But they had been knotted competently. He inhaled slowly and then cut off a liana with a well-aimed jet of fire. Suddenly one of the Pinks became restless. Sparkle interrupted his efforts instantaneously. He waited until all of them snored consistently again. He could easily release his second and his third leg. Just one more leg was left which he had to untie. All of a sudden one member of Charc's brigade started to stir. He tossed and turned until he finally got up to relieve himself. Then he curled up with a grunt and went back into sleep. Sparkle had frozen immediately. As soon as everything was quiet again he cut off the fourth liana. He disentangled himself with a yank from the burnt plant and then sneaked away as silently as possible towards the shore. He hesitated for a brief moment while considering which direction he should take. Slowly and noiselessly he slipped into the water and swam for his life, heading towards the east. He didn't know for how long he would be able to dive or swim. Neither did he know how long it would take him to reach dry land. But everything was better than waiting for The Red to return so that he could steal his stone and kill him. Sparkle dived under the surface and swam for his life.

Despite their rush to get home, Nero and Diane took a rest now and then. They were just sitting on a beach, of one of the isles in the southern sea, when Nero inquired,
"How did you find your arrow? Will you tell me that, dear warrior maid?"
Diane smiled and started to tell her story,
"When Charc and I reached the volcanic island, he was convinced that we had found the correct place. But I just had this gut feeling that he must have been mistaken.
I argued with him but in the end, I gave up. I thought if I can't find my stone, it might increase my chance to escape."
"I had already spotted you at that time."
"Really, did you? He sent me to explore the island in more detail, but I didn't see you at all."

"I had to stay hidden so that he wouldn't see me."

"The rest of the story you already know. It was you who showed me the way to the correct location. An island in various shades of grey with an open sinkhole. At a few spots hot smoke still emerged from different openings and cracks. I tried to alight but the surface burst. I burnt my little talon in the hot lava stream which flowed underneath the thin crust down into the ocean. I immediately got off the ground again. It was obvious that I had to pick up my jewel from out of the air. I circled around the island a few times. On the second sunrise when the sun shined diagonally onto the crater, it got reflected as a pitch-dark arrow. It began on the crater's edge and proceeded in a straight line directly down the hill. The tip of the arrow ended shortly before the coast, pointing towards the sea. I was absolutely convinced that the arrowhead indicated the direction to my gemstone. But I couldn't perch there. I would have burned my whole body. I pondered my next move. Finally, I had the idea. I had to try whether I could combat fire with fire. I was desperately hoping that my fire was already more intense than the volcano's. But at the same time, I had to be careful not to turn my own gem into magma.

"Impressive," Nero listened attentively.

"I decided not to start at once at the location where I assumed to find my stone. First, I wanted to practice somewhere else. I picked a spot which was a bit further away. It worked well. So, I flew back to the arrowhead. I carefully dosed my jet of fire, aimed at the tip of the arrow and released a stream of fire. Hot magma bubbled up through the crust which had opened up. And all of a sudden, I saw it. A stone got pushed outside by the hot lava right at the end of the arrow. It matched exactly the description which I had received. I stopped spitting fire, dashed towards the sea to cool my claws before getting it quickly out of the burning magma. Then I threw it into the water. Immediately I also dived in to fetch it again. Still in the water I plugged it into my dent. I felt my body tingling. And then I have become a mature dragon, fully and completely. Look! I am perfected, aren't I?"

"Yes Diane, you really are a warrior maid."

CHARC

The Red arrived full of evil energy at his retreat. He wanted to leave with Sparkle to get his gem instantaneously. His companions beat around the bush. But finally, they had to admit that Sparkle had been able to escape.

"YOU, USELESS PACK!"

His face twisted with rage.

"Can't I even leave you a dragon kid to look after? I don't want to know whose fault that was. But I'll make you pay for that."

"B.., b...but, we have a substitute."

"Your substitute can't be good enough to calm my anger. Get it over here," he hissed in anger.

Two of the Pink Brigade dragged Sandy in front of Charc.

"Well, if that isn't a coincidence! You are also one of them. I saw you at the Gathering."

Sandy was scared stiff by his deep voice and his massive body. And even worse, his red eyes with the dark pupils. She couldn't say a word.

"Can't you speak? Or don't you want to? Now you will see what happens if one doesn't follow Charc's instructions."

His rage needed an outlet. He whirled around in a flurry. His tremendous jet of fire caught one of the Brigade's members who at once went up in flames. The Red developed a taste for revenge and so he didn't stop shooting fire at his companion until nothing was left of him apart from his glowing rose quartz. Sandy was so shocked that she had forgotten to breathe. Even though the rest of the gang members were already used to his penalties all of them felt on edge, shrinking back, motionless. Everyone tried to avoid getting Charc's attention.

"I've lost two stones! What do you think, how will you make up for that?"

"But we have a dragon-girl. She hasn't been at the Oracle's."

"When did the bloody jerk disappear?"

The Pink didn't think for long. He didn't want to get incinerated.

"Not even five sunrises ago."

Although Sparkle had escaped more than twenty sunrises ago. His companions stared at him in surprise but Charc didn't notice that.

"Well, then I will look for the fur-creature in the far north, in the world of ice and snow. I will easily catch up with him. And you, baby, you will join me! Because after your brother, it will be your turn!"

DIANE, NERO AND SPARKLE

It had taken Diane and Nero more than thirty sunrises to get to Stella's cave. Nero had been pondering throughout the journey how he could gently break the news to his mother that he had heard from his brother but had lost contact again.

Stella welcomed them with a bright smile and pointed towards the cave.

"Come in. There is a little surprise waiting for you."

Nero entered. And here among all his brothers and sisters he saw Sparkle telling them his story.

"Sparkle! You've made it! You were able to escape!"

Sparkle jumped off the ledge where he had been sitting and gave Nero a big hug.

"Nero, I tried to contact you over and over again. But it was always in vain."

"I kept diving too in order to communicate with you. But I never got an answer from you."

"Sincere thanks to Adama! Now we are back together."

"You have to tell me how you were able to escape."

"Of course, I will. But let me finish first telling the others the end of my story."

Nero waited patiently. In the past he would have interrupted his brother insisting to hear the whole story.

"Well folks, I swam for my life. I hadn't known that I was able to swim such long distances non-stop. I pressed my wings against my body and just used my legs and claws. I was really fast when I practiced the crawl. One day land appeared on the horizon. You cannot imagine how delighted I was when I finally caught sight of it. I kept turning around to reassure myself that neither Charc nor one of his fellows had followed me. Even though, I felt pretty safe as I had given The Red the wrong direction. When I arrived on dryland, I firstly had to get my bearings. In front of me stretched an impenetrable tropical rainforest. I remembered that Aunt Bernie had told us about this dense jungle which was supposed to grow in the north of our cave and covered the main part of our continent. And then it was obvious. I instructed myself: Sparkle, you have to head to the south! This time I flew. After a few sunrises I eventually got back home."

"But how could you get rid of the Pink Brigade?"
Nero asked curiously.
"I will tell you that later on."
"Look, someone has accompanied me."
Sparkle didn't believe his eyes.
"Diane! And you have already got your jewel! Wow, it looks amazing! I've the impression you have a long story to tell us, too."
The excitement had to settle a bit before Nero noticed that Silent Wings and Sandy weren't present.
"Both of them are on their way to find their stones. And your father flew back to the Council of The Seven. Together they want to find a way how to defeat Charc at last."
"I am surprised to hear that. I didn't expect Sandy to be already mature enough to find her gem,"
Nero remarked.
Bernadette had to admit that Sandy had cheated her and then had followed Draco, Stella and Silent Wings to the Oracle.
"So, she is also on her way to seek her jewel."
That was the right moment for Rubi to inform her family,

"And this is exactly what I am going to do too during the next sunrises."
Turning to Sparkle Nero gathered,
"And we have to look for our new habitats. The Oracle sent the two of us towards the north. So, we might as well set off together. What exactly did the Oracle tell you? Where are you supposed to search?"
Sparkle repeated Adama's words,

"But your gem you will find underneath the scorching sun
Twinkling through the sweltering desert sand
Shining in all colors of the rainbow."

Stella knew only two vast deserts. One was located in the north the other one in the south of the continent.
"If I were you, I'd start to search here in the south desert, Hakan. If you aren't successful you can still fly to the north."
"That's what I will do."
Sparkle, Nero and Diane said goodbye to the ones who remained at home. Nero turned to Sparkle,
"My dear brother, wherever you are we'll stay in contact if possible."
"That's a good idea", Sparkle confirmed.

Rubi departed as well in order to receive her prediction. All of them left in different directions. Only Stella, Bernadette and Rocket stayed behind.

"When you leave us, it will be very quiet here,"

Stella smiled sadly at Rocket.

CHARC AND SANDY

Sandy noticed very quickly that she wasn't able to keep up with Charc. They had covered only a short distance before he was forced to take another break. He didn't like that at all.

"You are such a weakling. You can't be a dragon. I really have to make up my mind. Do I want to possess your stone?"

But the worst was still to come. As soon as they reached the ice desert Sandy collapsed. The frostiness had stiffened her limbs. Her body was numb, her skin covered by ice. And when a fierce blizzard caught them, she gave up completely. She plunged down to the ground where she crouched in the snow on a thick sheet of ice and waited to die. Charc didn't want to allow that. Not because of empathy or helpfulness. No, these were unknown words to him. But because he needed each and every gem so that he could become the undisputed master of the dragons as soon as possible. He already possessed the black diamond. A stone which even the Oracle had on its forehead; just without the inclusions. And the Oracle was the most powerful dragon in their world. The bloodstones of Charc's victims enhanced his skills. Without these he wouldn't have been so skillful. He just had to find the remaining gems in order to become invincible. And that was why he needed this little wimp. He had to provide shelter for her. He alighted behind her and spread his huge wings with which he covered Sandy's body so that she was protected from the biting winds and the piercing snow crystals. By the time the storm disappeared he had made his decision.

"We are going to find shelter for you where you will wait for me until I've found your brother. Got it?"

Sandy barely reacted. She was alive but frozen to the bone and quite stiff. She starred at the tip of her tail. The icy temperatures had deadened it.

"What's that?" She started to cry.

"Now she is crying. Incredible! Pull yourself together! Here take some dragon-skin-powder. It'll help you."

Sandy felt on top of the world again. Now she would be able to manage another long-distance flight.

"We're leaving."

The powder had released new energies. Charc had been giving her drugs and had slowly increased the dosage. One never knew when one would need a submissive dragon-lady. He was still focused on getting her stone but that could change. Maybe he could make other use of her. The Red approached a small elevation in the middle of this endless ice desert. He started to dig up the downwind side of it until he got through the outer layer of ice. Underneath a little miracle appeared. The bottom was covered by a steaming pool. The rising warm air had smoothened the walls and had turned their color into a translucent light-blue.

"You are staying right here until I pick you up again. Got it? Warm yourself up slowly in the warm water. Then you will soon feel better. But don't leave the hole."

Sandy did what Charc had told her. She slowly slipped into the warm water to soothe her body. But somehow, she had the distinct impression that someone or something was constantly watching her.

DRACO

Draco headed as quickly as possible to the seat of the Council. The "Council of the Seven Stones" consisted of wise dragons who administered justice, punished culprits and handled irreconcilable disputes.

Its members were sent from different habitats. Draco was the intermediary between Adama and The Wise. Chochop was the representative of the air. Hinto came from the deep dark blue sea in order to represent the interests of those inhabitants. Hakana was a typical desert dweller. Whereas Yas represented the interests of the snowcapped mountains and the ice deserts. Adahy's family lived in the dense jungle. Only the representative of the galaxies was still missing. The Council had to be complete and all gemstones had to be combined. Without him the Council was unable to have the absolute power. Which didn't mean that they were allowed to harm any other dragon. The primary guidance was:

Never kill your equals.

Charc had sinned against this law. He had to be punished for that.

Although the Council had already been holding its meeting for an entire sunrise they still hadn't come to an agreement.

"Even if we had the power and the strength to kill him, it would be unjustified. We would break our first and most important law."

Hakana was outraged,

"I think we should track him down. Together we will be so much stronger than him. And then he should be exiled to a remote world."

Draco remarked,

"You seem to be forgetting that our Council is just missing that very dragon who would be able to do that, to get him outside of our world."

"Well."

"We have to get him before he causes even more harm. Put him in a secure place, he can't escape from."

Hinto already had a place in mind.

"Shouldn't we seek Adama's advice?" Draco interfered.

"Let's cast a vote!" Chochop looked from one member to the other.

As everybody agreed, Draco set off again to see the Oracle.

DIANE AND NERO, CHARC AND SANDY

Diane and Nero hovered leisurely above The Green Canopy of the Great Jungle. Then they turned towards the north and finally returned to Draco's homeland.

"We aren't very far from my place of birth. But now I am grown up and I am going to find my own habitat,"

explained Diane.

Nero took notice of this without any comment.

They traversed estuaries and rested on little islands. The weather grew harsh. But both of them enjoyed the cold damp air and the strong winds. One sunrise Nero saw a crème-colored dragon resting in a tiny cove.

After The Red had to admit that his undertaking had been completely useless, he had returned to the ice cave to pick Sandy up. Together they flew towards the south. They were just taking a rest in this little cove when he saw two dragons approaching them.

"We are having visitors. Be quiet."

"Why? This is my brother Nero. I recognize him because of his orange underbelly. The other dragon I've never seen before."

"Well, I have," Charc grunted.

"I'll hide in the undergrowth. And you will find out, from your brother, where the little fur-creature is staying. I still have a bone to pick with him. And don't try anything! I'll be watching. If you are nice and obedient you will get more of the dragon-powder. Got it?"

"Yeah, sure."

Sandy had already reached a stage which only allowed her to think from one dosage to the next. What might happen to her brother didn't interest her anymore.

"I can't believe it! Diane, look! That is my sister Sandy down there."

"Well, let's perch there, shall we?"

Diane and Nero headed towards Sandy and alighted next to her.

"Sandy what are you doing here? Mum told us that you are looking for your gem. But Adama hasn't even given you your mark."

"Yes, I was at the Oracle's. But I was told to come back later."

"Why that?"

"I don't know."

"And what are you doing here?"

"I am trying to find my stone without the prophecies. But we are talking far too much about me. What about you?"

"Oh, by the way, this is Diane. The Red had kidnapped her but we were able to escape and we've found her gem."

"Interesting stone. And what about Sparkle? Do you know anything about him?"

"Yes, of course. That was terrific! Charc had captivated Sparkle. But he could escape. He had given The Red the wrong location where to find his jewel. This way he gained a lot of time. Now he is looking for his gem in the Hakan Desert."

"When has he left?"

"Well, maybe around fifteen sunrises ago. We departed all at the same time."

"Then he should have found his jewel by now."

"I don't think so,"

Nero doubted.

"The Oracles instructions were rather ambiguous. What about you Sandy, do you want to accompany us?"

"No, no Nero. I am staying here for some time and then I am going to fly back to Adama, since I was told to return."

"Fine. Then we will continue our journey."
Diane and Nero spread their wings and flapped away.
Sandy waited until she couldn't see them any longer.
"You may come out. The coast is clear. They are gone."
"Good girl,"
Charc already savored his victory.
"And now tell me what is the news?"

Diane and Nero had been soaring silently through the air for some time when Diane remarked,
"Your sister is a bit peculiar, isn't she?"
"I've just thought the same. That was strange. We hadn't seen each other for such a long time. She didn't even mention my stone. She was only interested in Sparkle. Diane, it was all about Sparkle! There is something odd going on. Let's turn around and see whether she is really heading to the Oracle."
Diane and Nero made a U-turn. This time they glided closely above the trees to conceal themselves.

"Nero, look over there! I will never forget this dragon in my entire life. It's Charc! And he is hurtling with your sister to the south!"

"She desperately wanted to know where Sparkle is, how long he has been gone and so on. Diane, I've revealed every detail about my brother. These two are on their way to the Hakan Desert!"

"We'll track them. Maybe Sparkle has already found his gem and The Red will arrive too late."

It was easy to follow them as long as they hadn't reached the desert. They stayed hidden behind clouds, tall trees or high mountains. But there was nowhere to hide in the plains of the desert. They were forced to stay further behind in order to stay out of sight.

And in the end, they had lost them.

Sparkle couldn't believe his eyes. He had finally found his gemstone. Sunrise after sunrise he had been scanning the desert. He had been looking for something shining in the bleak mountains as well as in the hot dunes, which he had discovered during a sand storm. In the end it was pure coincidence that he was successful. Hunger and thirst had gnawed at his throat. His tongue had felt swollen. It probably had been twice the size as normal.

"I will stay one more sunrise in this desert but then I'll move on,"

he thought by himself. He was just taking a rest in the shade of a rock and as he grew bored, he started to roll some stones down the hill. He watched them leaping downhill. Suddenly his attention got caught by a bright twinkle. What had Adama said?

"But your gem you will find underneath
the scorching sun
twinkling through the sweltering desert
sand
shining in all colors of the rainbow."

He jumped up and fell almost down the hill. Between the grey rocks hid a white stone. Its inclusions blazed in the most dazzling colors of the rainbow. He removed it carefully from the rock and tried to insert it into his mark on his head. Lightning-quick it had adjusted itself, a brief tingling ran through his body which turned him into a mature dragon; he felt a kind of completeness, wholeness.

But suddenly two claws packed him, coming from above. Charc and Sandy had seen him inserting his stone into his forehead. The Red couldn't suppress an evil smile,

"Finally, I got you, you bloody fool. This will be a horrible time for you."

He was determined to have his revenge now.

"I can't remember how often I was told how marvelous your grand-father and your father were. And I have always been the good-for-nothing. This will be the price for my pain which I had to endure throughout my entire youth."

Sparkle was so shocked. He didn't understand what The Red was talking about.

"Well, you may run and run, little wimp. You won't get away. I will make you suffer for wasting my precious time!"

Sparkle kicked vigorously and tried to escape, but to no avail. Defeat became unavoidable. Charc enjoyed Sparkle's helplessness.

"Well, you little fur-creature, I want to have real fun. This will be torture time now."

The Red made his black diamond glow and a thin beam hit the rock next to Sparke.

The stone melted immediately. A small trickle of melted rocks dripped like water down the mountain.

"Get over here, you lazy ass. You can help me!"

It was only now that Sparkle noticed his sister Sandy.

"Sandy what are you doing here at his side?"

"I, I, I …"

"Tell him, that it was you who has betrayed him. You have a lovely sister, fur-creature! But I will fill her days with agony, too."

Charc started to loosen Sparkle's stone with a beam emitted from his gem. Sparkle tried to be brave. But when the third beam hit him, he was half blind with pain. He curled on the ground and fainted. Suddenly two dark dragons plunged down onto Charc. Nero clung fast around Charc's head. His sharp claws pierced into his eyes, ears and nose.

"Diane, take care of Sparkle, will you?"

Charc snarled, struggled and gathered his strengths. He shook himself and managed easily to release himself from Nero's iron grip. But Diane possessed the rainbow-obsidian, the arrow of the warrior. She wouldn't give up so quickly. Out of her mouth shot an enormous jet of fire which was followed by a stream of bundled flashes coming from her stone. The Red was stunned.

"I knew your gems are valuable. Yours is lost for me but I'll get the little bloody bastard's!"

"I wouldn't be so sure about that. Are you able to handle grown-ups as well, or only kids and adolescents?"

The Red was addressed roughly from behind.

He whirled around in a flurry and faced Draco, who cocked his beard and took a step towards him.

The Red felt cornered. He would get another chance some other time. But now his only opportunity was to escape. He stepped backwards, took off and then twisted through the air.

"Daddy, daddy, shall we follow him? And by the way, where did you come from?"

"That isn't important at the moment, Nero. Right now, we have to look after Sparkle."

Sandy was just about to sneak away but Draco's deep voice kept her from leaving.

"Sandy you stay here and tell us how you got into this mess."

Diane was already next to Sparkle. He was still unconscious. His wound was bleeding profusely.

"Someone has to take care of his wounds. We need a healer to get him out of the coma. We should take him to Stella."

Turning to Sandy, he sharply ordered,

"And you are coming with us!"

Draco placed Sparkle's limp body, with his belly up, onto his own powerful front claws. "Diane, you are staying with me. Nero and Sandy, you fly to Stella's cave as fast as possible and tell her what has happened. She shall prepare everything she needs so that she can take care of Sparkle. Nero, keep a keen eye on Sandy. Don't let her mess up again."

"Sure."

Nero took off, followed by Sandy who felt deeply ashamed.

"Come on Diane. We will also set off. You'll stay behind me and make sure we won't be attacked by this bastard again."

Draco and Diane had to break their journey several times as the extra weight of Sparkle's body slowed him down.

Draco struggled to continue flying and finally, after a few sunrises, they reached Stella's den. Bernadette was heartbroken. "This all wouldn't have happened if I had told you earlier. But it hadn't occurred to me at all that he might be so unscrupulous to kidnap the young dragons right at the Assembly. And I just couldn't talk about it. My agony was so immense,"
she uttered in despair.
"Bernie, we cannot turn the time back. Now it is important to focus on Sparkle's health,"
Stella pointed out.
"Yes, of course, you are right."
Stella and Bernadette helped Draco to carry Sparkle into the den where Draco lowered him to the ground. Various dragon-skin-powders had been prepared by his mother in the meantime.
Draco had already given her some of his own ground skin when being at the Assembly. He seldom molted anymore. But as he was aware of Stella's skills how to use the skin efficiently, he had given it to her. His ground skin was able to heal any kind of physical deficiency. Rubi's powder on the other hand had revitalizing power.

"I'll try giving him a mixture of yours and Rubi's skin,"

Stella explained Draco.

"I'll need some water in order to prepare a paste."

Sandy volunteered immediately to get water but Draco gave her a piercing look and hold her back.

"You fetch nothing. You'll stay here under observation,"

he ordered and then turned to Stella.

"The young lady is going to tell us later on why The Red might still be able to kidnap Sparkle."

Meekly Sandy withdrew herself into the last corner of the cave.

With the help of a leaf, Rocket carried some water to Stella. She mixed it to make a paste out of it and rubbed it on the wound. Sparkle groaned quietly. Stella didn't know whether it was out of pain or relief. Even though, Draco had covered the wound with styptic leaves the bloodstream couldn't be stopped.

All they could do was to renew the paste, sit at his side and wait.

After a few sunrises the wound slowly healed but Sparkle was still unconscious. Stella tried to get him out of the coma with

some of her own skin which she had ground. It helped to purify one's soul. Maybe it would also help Sparkle.
But even after applying it for numerous times, all efforts were in vain. Stella turned to Draco,
" I have only one idea left. We'll need one of Adama's scales."
"I'll try getting it."
Draco resumed his journey to the Oracle which he had interrupted in order to save his son's life.

Before Draco set off for his journey to Adama, Sandy had to account for her actions.
"Where shall I start? With my feeling of inferiority which I have had since early childhood?"
whispered Sandy, weakly.
"I just wanted to be as competent as the others."
Stella felt sympathy for her daughter. She said softly,
"But you know, my dear, some take longer to mature than others. That is absolutely normal. You just needed a bit more time," she reassured her daughter.

"Mum, I am so sorry what I've done. But when the Oracle told me that I wasn't mature enough I was completely devastated. And that is why I got involved with the Pink Brigade and The Red. He gave me lots of dragon-skin-powder. And I did everything for him to please him so that I would get even more of it."

"Do you know where Charc is hiding?"

"Yes, I do."

"That is good news. Although I don't think that this vicious troublemaker is still there. He has definitely looked for another hiding place,"

Draco weighed the odds.

"But the most important thing is Sparkle's recovery right now. We have to do anything and everything to get him out of the coma,"

Stella said to Bernadette and Sandy.

"Nero, you and Diane, you have to fly to my mother to get more dragon-skin-powder as I am running low especially on Rubi's. And you Sandy, you will also get a treatment which will boost your self-confidence. Then you won't need any drugs anymore."

Thus, Draco made his way to the Oracle while Nero and Diane headed to Grandmother Raiffa.

"Sandy, you take care of Sparkle. Take turns with Aunt Bernadette. I hope, you won't mess up again."

"No Mum, of course not. I won't cause any more troubles."

Despite Sandy's promise, everybody who remained in the cave, kept an eye on her, that was Stella, Bernadette and Rocket. But Sandy felt upright remorseful. She devotedly looked after Sparkle. She moved him in different positions, drenched him healing potion, told him his pranks dating back to their childhood and begged him over and over again to forgive her. Tears slid down her face and across his scar which had only just closed. But not even these tears helped him to regain consciousness.

RUBI

"You are the blood of the earth
emerged from the interior
millions of rotations ago
born to heal
You are going to find your divine purpose
While looking for your cup
no warm light will accompany you
no cold light will support you
only your inner eye can help you
to find your stone."

Rubi was puzzled. The Oracle hadn't given her any directions. The dent, caused by Adama's golden scale, wasn't of any help either. It just looked like a bowl.
"What is that supposed to mean?"
She left Adama's cliff.
"That is most ridiculous. I don't know where to fly to. And I have a bowl-shaped mark in my head."
It had always been Ruby's wish to see the endless ocean. As she had already heard various stories from Draco, Stella, Bernadette and then from Nero, Sparkle and Diane, her interest had constantly increased. Since she hadn't received any

directions she decided, that she might as well fly to the endless blue water.

She reached the shore of the ocean right after sun set. The silver disk of the Cold Light reflected off the pitch-dark surface. It didn't make any difference in which direction Rubi turned, the shining light accompanied her everywhere. Even though this was really fascinating, it wouldn't help her to find her jewel. She perched on a cliff at the edge of the lagoon from where she had a breathtaking view unto the shimmering surface. With open eyes inner pictures arose.

She saw herself, crossing the deep blue water until she reached the continent with the name of Chendris. A massive mountain range towered up towards the sky right in front of her. She had only just seen the green grassland and forests in the valleys, now she was facing cliffs which became more rugged and inhospitable the further she soared up into the air. Above the snow- and ice-covered mountains she was barely able to breathe anymore. With her last strength she crossed the peaks. But then, on the north-facing slope, a gust of wind caught her and she plummeted downward toward the ground.

Rubi shivered. Relieved she noticed that she was still at the edge of the lagoon at the shore of the deep blue water.

"Sincere thanks to Adama! But maybe that's my guidance. I will travers the deep blue sea when the sun rises and then I will decide what to do next. How long did it take Sparkle? I am sure it will take at least fifteen sunrises to get there."

During her flight Rubi considered various possibilities how to avoid the danger of the mountains.

"Maybe I can fly around them? But as I don't know the direction, how am I supposed to know how to veer away from them? I could slowly climb into the sky so that I can adapt to the height and avoid exhaustion."

She decided to carry on flying, "I can deal with that when the time comes."

Rubi had reached the shore of an island after a long journey. A range of untamed mountains rose up to the sky. She glided down to rest in a little cove. As soon as she crouched low to the ground, she immediately fell asleep. Nightmares haunted her again.

She was facing menacing mountains which she attempted to cross, but to no avail. The air grew thinner and thinner. When she thought that she had finally reached the highest peak another steep mountain range appeared behind the first one. And the following one was even higher than the previous one. They stretched on and on. Eventually she woke up completely bewildered.

"Will I find my gem in these dreadful mountains? No! Definitely not!"

After she had calmed down again and stilled her hunger, she continued her voyage. When she reached the snowcapped peaks of the tremendous mountains, by contrast to her dreams, she was able to see the sparkling blue water in the far distance. This is where she headed to. According to the stories, her siblings had told her, she knew, the continent Chendris would appear behind the straits. In the south lay a tropical rainforest while towards the north the temperature dropped continuously. Miles of steep cliffs edged the coastline. They were called The Invisible Summits because they were constantly blocked from view by the clouds. Nobody really knew how far they towered up into the sky. After three sunrises Rubi arrived at the banks of Chendris. She perched on a cliff in a little cove and started to meditate. She looked as if she was made out of stone. But after coming out of trance again she knew her way.

"I am going to fly around the mountains, along the shore. That will lead me towards north-west and then I will enter deep into the inner part of the continent."

Pleased to have found a preliminary direction Rubi continued her journey. She came to the western part of the mountain range after three further sunrises. The majestic mountains started to flatten until they became gently rolling hills. Rubi took another rest. She satisfied her hunger and then turned towards north-east into the heart of the country. Wasteland covered this part of the continent made up of bleak plateaus with mountains of average height. Herds of wild horses populated the prairie. Once and again she caught one of the horses. After three further sunrises she broke her journey again. She glanced around. Knee-high dry grass stretched across a huge plain that extended to the distant horizon and fused into the sky. And again, did she settle into her meditation-position which she had already got used to. Looking like a dragon-statue with closed eyes and an erected head she started her reflection. She tried to sooth her mind.

Inner pictures slowly started to emerge. The wavy grass blades of the steppe led her towards a ravine which was edged by steep rugged cliffs on both sides. She was led even further into the gorge. The jagged rocks became steeper and steeper until she eventually faced an unscalable wall.

"I am a dragon! I can fly!"

But her inner eye showed her that she wouldn't be able to overcome the obstacle by flying. She started to dig; further and faster. She struggled hard. First, she broke up the soil with her forelegs and then pushed it towards her rear legs. With her rear legs she pawed the piles towards the back from where she removed the soil with powerful strokes out of her way. Then she started the same procedure all over again. Rubi didn't know how much time she had spent doing her meditating. But she was convinced to know what she had to do. She took off and soared above the wasteland. In the far distance she recognized an elevation which she targeted. She had to search for quite some time until she finally found an opening in the cliff which resembled the ravine she had seen in her mind's eye. But there it was! Edged by steep rugged cliffs on both sides it led far into the interior of the rock. Rubi continued flying consistently. But then the canyon became narrower. She had to decide whether to leave the canyon again without getting to the end of it or to glide down onto the ground.

"I will try to reach the wall, which traverses the gorge, on foot."

Rubi glided down and started crawling on all fours along the trail.

"For a dragon like me this is most embarrassing."

The sun had already set a long time ago. Only the cold light of the silver disk revealed the trail when suddenly a blustery gust of wind howled through the night, a speck drifted in front of the silver disk of the Cold Light, and left her in the intense darkness of the ravine, obscuring her path. Rubi continued her way. What had the Oracle said?

"While looking for your cup

no warm light will accompany you
no cold light will support you
Only your inner eye can help you
to find your stone."

She reached the wall and started to dig as she had seen it in her mind's eye. She labored dragonlenght after dragonlenght underneath the cliff. Her eyes were closed. She only paid attention to her instinct and reacted accordingly. She had problems breathing as the fine dust blocked her nostrils. All of a sudden, she felt something hard. With her front claws she dug it out of the stone and with the support of her rear legs she was able to move it further out.
"I have to have a break."
With a last powerful stroke, she shot the hard thing out of the passageway. A rumbling and a clanking noise followed which raised her curiosity. She moved quickly backwards out of the ditch. The cool light had returned. Rubi surveyed her surroundings.
"What's that?"
Embedded in white crystals something red gleamed. Rubi took a closer look. It had the form of her mark. Carefully she took it into her front claws and tried to scratch the

white crystals off the red stone, but without any success. There was only one possibility left. She put the stone on the ground and with a well-aimed jet of fire she separated the ruby from the worthless crystal; at least that was what she presumed it was. Then she placed the bowl-shaped gem onto her forehead. As everybody else had already experienced it before, a tingling ran through her body and her gemstone came alive.

"But I still don't know why I'm carrying a bowl on my head."

Adama had given her this answer in the first part of her prophecy:

"You are the blood of the earth
emerged from the interior
millions of rotations ago
Born to heal
you are going to find your divine purpose"

Rubi didn't hesitate long. She was born to heal. Maybe she could help her brother. She had to head for home immediately.

SILENT WINGS

Silent Wings had already surveyed the isle attentively from above. While descending she had a hunch that she had reached her destination This was the Island of the Damned. The creatures who lived here were unable to fly. Their lifestyle and their appearance had adapted to the island's environment. They walked around on their hind legs while their forelegs were stunted. This way it was easier for them to make their way quickly through the dense woods. Due to the small size of the isle and the tight food availability the dragons who lived here had become cannibals over many thousand rotations. Their strongest weapon were their giant fangs in their enormous mouths. Many of these beasts had deformations due to incest. Other disorders like bone loss, mental deterioration and many other symptoms weren't noticeable but they also existed. Silly felt as if she was watched.

"Oh Adama, how am I supposed to get out of here alive?"

She decided, she would start her search by discovering the area. She left the clearing and advanced into the thick forest. Conifers with wide overhanging branches and long filigreed needles grew tightly to one another. Fallen trees made it even harder for her to cut her way through the wood. It was nearly impossible to get through the forest as it got increasingly thicker. And the entire time she had the feeling that someone was staring at her.

"This doesn't make sense at all. I cannot scan the entire island on all four legs. Neither can I burn it down."

Silly decided to return to the clearing and to explore the island from above. She would look for a landmark where her stone might be hidden. She was just struggling across another pile of fallen trees when suddenly one of the native creatures barred her way. It straightened itself to reach its full stature and threatened her with its razor-sharp teeth. Silent Wings tried to soothe him, tried to communicate that she neither wanted to claim territory nor food.

"It doesn't understand a word. But we aren't allowed to kill any dragons," she pondered desperately.

The creature pawed the ground. It turned in a side-on position to take a fast run-up.

Then it attacked her. Silly's thoughts were spinning around in her head.

"It is strictly prohibited to kill dragons! But I don't want to get killed either. What shall I do?"

And suddenly the only option left was crystal clear. She drew herself up and stood tall and straight, cocked her beard, gaped and released a gigantic jet of fire which she placed right in front of her opponent's feet. The beast paused in astonishment. But since it hadn't been hurt by the fire, it made a second attempt to attack her. Silly aimed at its legs. She was trying to immobilize the beast so that she would have a chance to escape. The creature cursed and howled in rage and agony. She had obviously achieved her goal. With her wings pressed tightly to her body she crashed through the dense forest. Branches cut her face, with her shoulders she bumped into trees and behind her she could hear wood cracking under its huge claws. When she reached the clearing, she could already feel its breath. Two, three steps then she took off and flapped away above the tree tops of the forest. Underneath her she could hear the enemy hissing in anger.

"The island is packed with these beasts. How can I possibly find my gemstone here?" Silent Wings circled the isle looking for another spot where to land. But this time different criteria had to be met. She had to make sure that her secret retreat couldn't be reached by any of these creatures. A place where she could rest in safety. It should serve her as a starting point from where she could continue her search for her protective stone. Eventually she discovered a hollow in the cliffs far above the ocean. She examined it immediately. Bones of small animals, which had been able to fly, were scattered across the ground. Silly inspected the place more closely. Her retreat was large enough so that she could comfortably sleep in it without any disturbances.

Silent Wings thought feverishly how she should be able to find her gemstone on this island. She had already discovered two hills which looked promising. But even these were densely wooded which would cause her major problems. The trees stood too close. She needed a forest aisle without any trees otherwise she wouldn't be able to alight safe and sound. Of course, she could cut an aisle into the thick forest with her powerful dragon fire. But the forest would go up in flames; uncontrolled and dangerous. The dragon codex forbade the usage of the jet of fire, unless one was in direct danger. Deliberately killing living beings was also prohibited.

"But this is exactly what would happen in this case. I wouldn't have any control how far the fire would spread. The dry twigs and the fallen trees on the ground they are going to burn like tinder. I can't take the risk. I might burn the whole isle. I have to come up with another idea."

And again, Silent Wings skimmed over the two hills in order to determine the best approach path.

"No clearing. Nothing. I could try to perch on a strong branch. And from there I could attempt to climb down from one branch to another. But then I will face the danger again to be attacked by one of those creatures. The only option left, if I had to escape, would be to climb back up again. I'll give it a try."

Silent Wings started on the northern side of one of the hills. The forested hills dropped steeply down into the sea. No hollows were to be seen which could offer her shelter.

She headed towards a majestic cedar where she wanted to land. She had circled around the tree for a few times before she decided which branch to use. Shortly before she reached the top of the tree she pressed her wings against her body, stretched her legs to the front so that she could grip the branch.

"Wow, made it!"

The cedar swayed and Silly waited until the tree steadied again before climbing it down. When she touched the ground, she surveyed her surrounding to reassure herself.

"First of all, I have to clear this place so that I can dig without any disturbances."

She was constantly alert to suspicious noises or the absence of these; which also could mean danger when she began to do her work.

"For one dragon that is quite a lot of work."

The sun was about to set when she finally climbed up the cedar again and returned to her hiding place.

She labored and dug through the rubble for numerous sunrises. The opening grew larger. But at the same time the risk of collapsing increased too. She hadn't come across a single gem yet. One sunrise,

Silly hadn't dug for long, when a rumbling sound suddenly came to her ears.

"My passage is collapsing! I've to get out of here."

Silent Wings crawled as quickly as possible out of her mine. When she got outside of it she was surrounded by an unknown silence. She looked to the sea. But the sea was gone. With a searching gaze she checked the area to make sure that no native inhabitant of the Isle of the Damned was nearby. She couldn't see any. Feeling secure she wanted to continue digging. That was the moment when the disaster hit the island. A blustering noise cut through the silence coming from the ocean. Silent Wings turned around. A huge wave came rolling up to the isle and herself. She spun around and fled towards the cedar and trying to climb up the tree. It was a desperate race against time. The water increased at a tremendous speed. Silly kept climbing up the tree in the hope of being able to escape. The tidal wave reached the isle and along with it came piles of rocks, debris and trees. These caused the cedar to go down in less than no time. Silly was torn down into the depth of the floods. She frantically fought against the drift of the water, but to no avail.

"What is that?"

Silent Wings had caught a glimpse of a sparkling hexagon in the water while drowning. She stretched out her claw, grabbed it and clung to it tightly. Then her vision clouded and she blacked out.

When Silent Wings slowly rallied from the coma, pain was penetrating her entire body. She had been injured everywhere. She tried to raise her head. Well, at least that was possible. But through her right wing raced an explosion of agony. The tips of her wings stuck out awkwardly. And it caused her unbearable pain.

"What's that?"

Silent Wings stared at her left claw in which she firmly clemped a gemstone.

"A clear pure blue-colored six-sided prism. This must be my gem."

Carefully, she put the stone on the ground and examined her dent.

"It might fit!"

She inserted the stone into her mark. And her body tingled.

"I can't believe it. I've actually found my protective stone! And now?"

She looked around. She was standing on a beach surrounded by cliffs and debris, broken trees, dead fish and...and dead natives of the Island of the Damned.

"Oh dear, I am still on this island! I've to leave this place immediately,"

she concluded in sudden alarm.

Silent Wings gritted her teeth and then tried to raise herself. She winced with pain while trying to take a run-up in order to soar into the air. Impossible. Her right wing stuck out at an odd angle.

"I need a slight elevation from where I can take off. I just have to get away from this isle."

When the flood wave had hit the shore with its devastating force it had swept away all the trees, which had been in the lower half of the hill. Silent Wings started to climb up the slope.

"I assume that, under these circumstances, our codex doesn't apply. I will burn a swath into the rubble so that I can advance more quickly."

While struggling to the tree line, she ceaselessly prayed to Adama that no indigenous creature would appear. Silent Wings turned towards the ocean and started to run. Her swath, which was still fuming, gave her enough room to take a run-up.

"I am taking off now."

She clenched her teeth, started to run and spread her wings, which sent an explosion of agony through her body. Using the upwind, she struggled to gain altitude. She drifted towards the right. Barely staying above the water surface she was able to leave the island.

"Only Adama knows where I'll arrive."

Silly was extremely concerned.

SPARKLE

Sparkle felt ill at ease in his own skin. He was lying flat on his back. A position that made a dragon feel completely helpless. The bright sunlight blinded him. And all of a sudden, he was racing through a translucent tunnel right into space. Billions of stars passed him at a tearing pace. At the end of the tunnel he had to solve various problems of which he couldn't solve a single one. He noticed that he was disembodied. He was just his own spirit, without the weight of his body, moving through space. Even though, he still felt like a complete being. Suddenly a tremendous gate appeared in front of him. Gleaming bright light emerged through its cracks. An inner voice asked him,

"Sparkle, would you like to enter through this gate?"

He felt very tempted to walk through it. The closer he came the stronger got the temptation and a feeling of bliss forced him to keep walking. But Sparkle decided against it.

"No, I want to be myself. I still have so many things to do in our dragon-world."

The gate vanished and Sparkle blacked out.

He was obsessed by scattered nightmares. Sometimes he came briefly out of the coma but fainted again shortly afterwards. He felt drained of willpower. Neither Charc's poison nor the fear of getting captured again had left his body. Sparkle felt his pain just like through a haze. Fortunately, the pain slowly subsided. His visible wounds had begun to heal and his burnt hair had grown again. A broad scar was left next to his gemstone stretching down to his snout. Sandy and Bernadette treated it with a paste made of dragon-skin-powder and a juice made of dragon-root. It was supposed to prevent the tissue from hardening and to keep it smooth. Sparkle was able to sense the presence of dragons who treated him kindly. Gradually he recovered. After sixty sunrises he opened his eyes for the first time. At first, he neither knew where he was nor what had happened. The time period between Charc's attack and the arrival in his mother's cage had completely slipped his mind. And even the time afterwards he remembered only in a dreamy haze; just the short moments when he was conscious and when he was able to realize being in Stella's cave. But even these memories were rather dull. Slowly he moved his eyes. But his consciousness still didn't come back to him entirely.

ROCKET

"My time has come."
The last time when Rocket had performed his vertical take-off, he was able to shoot himself further into space than ever before. His decision to go to the Oracle was made. In contrast to his siblings he spiraled himself up into the atmosphere, moved himself counterclockwise with light flaps and then plunged down on the egg-shaped rock in the middle of Adama's territory.

"Magic, fire and electric conductivity
are going to support the Council of the
Seven
Since you are going to radiate flashes of
light
and spit fire
the long-awaited is you
The silver-shining dices of your stone
you are going to find
in perfect order
on one of the islands just off the coast
of the north continent
You are going to be a wanderer between
the worlds
You'll be able

to save your race
to find hidden memories
to explore foreign galaxies
while discovering the origin of the dragon
world
Travelling from one world to the other
your gem is going to accompany you
A member of the Council of the Seven
you are going to be
if your cube-shaped titanium
allows you to do so."

These were the Oracle's words for Rocket. He also got a mark on his forehead by one of Adama's ventral scales. He felt a tingling sensation and then found himself standing alone on the cliff. Rocket remembered seeing an island which was just off the north continent. This should be his destination. Rocket dashed into the air and kept to the north-west. Shortly after, he could already prepare his landing on that very isle.

Rocket perched high up on a plateau in the middle of the isle. This place resembled a pulpit. He was sitting at the edge of the precipice which plunged down thousands

of dragon-lengths. From this outlook he could enjoy a breathtaking view onto his surroundings. A river had divided the rock into two pieces which now snaked around the bold cliffs deep underneath him.
Rocket mused,
"Had the river already cut itself through the rocks before the dragons arrived on this planet? That would be interesting to know."
He surveyed the area with poise. He overlooked arid plains. A few brownish hills lay scattered in the distance. Each sunrise Rocket started to explore the island. And each sunset he returned unsuccessful to this starting point. He examined the remote hills; He dug deep into debris and rubble in order to find his gem. Nothing.
"Have I overlooked anything? The location is correct. What am I doing wrong?"
Rocket surged into the sky to have a better overview. But that didn't provide any meaningful guidance either. Tired and disappointed he settled again on his pulpit. While watching the sunset in the west he was pondering his situation when he suddenly noticed, out of the corner of his left eye, a gleam in the precipitous rock face. But when he turned his head, to take a closer look, the sun was down. The gleam

had vanished. At the next sun rise he had positioned himself in front of the rock face again, where he had seen the glow. Nothing. During the next sunrises he kept trying to find something that at least roughly resembled a gem.

"Am I really at the right spot? Should I return to the Oracle? No! I am staying here until I've found my stone."

And again, Rocket placed himself in front of the steep face. One sunset, while he was gazing at the steep wall underneath the pulpit, the entire rock suddenly glowed. He raised himself into the air to examine this phenomenon. But the sun had already set again. Night was falling.

"The next sunrise will bring the answer."

Rocket returned to his ledge and tried to fall asleep. But his eager anticipation deterred him from sleeping. With the first ray of sunshine he lifted himself into the air and inspected the wall bit by bit. For a long time, he didn't find anything. But all of a sudden, a dark-grey square blazed from the middle of the rock. Rocket touched his mark.

"But I've three square cylinders. I've to find those."

With a searching gaze he scanned the steep face over and over again. But somehow, he felt mesmerized by the first square which he had found.

"I'll try to get it out of the rock."

Rocket scratched carefully between the grey cylinder and the rock. The rock was stone-hard.

"I'll have to have lots of patience. By the time I get the gem out, I'll be as old as the hills."

Rocket kept scraping and his determined persistence got rewarded. After many sunrises he noticed a second cylinder which was attached to the first one. It lay a bit deeper inside the rock. This fueled his hopes again. He started scratching on the opposite side of the first cylinder. And he was successful. A third stone appeared. It was exactly on the same height as the second one. Rocket touched his dent.

"Hooray! I've found it! I just need a bit more patience. And then I'll have it."

But it was more than "a bit more patience". Rocket kept scratching and scraping at the rock until his claws were sore. One was chipped and blood dribbled down. But it had to be done. He had to get these three stones. These were the ones that fitted perfectly into his dent.

"I don't give up. And if I have to stay here forever."

One sunrise the time has finally come. The three-piece stone started to loosen. Very carefully he continued working on it. He almost got it. Nothing could go wrong anymore. Fortune smiled on Rocket. After a few sunrises he was able to take his three-part pyrite out of the cliff. He carried it up onto his pulpit and examined it attentively. Three squared cylinders had grown together to form one unit. Two of them lay a bit behind the other. Rocket touched its dent again. Dismay swept through him. His protective stone was supposed to consist of four parts.

"That just can't be true. I'm not supposed to start all over again, am I?"

He fingered his dent once again with meticulous precision. The fourth cuboid was underneath the two parts which were connected next to each other.

"Rocket, don't give up. After all, you had such a positive gut feeling."

He tried to encourage himself. And started scratching where he assumed to find the fourth cuboid. His patience got rewarded.

After an endless time, he spotted a dark-grey edge gleaming inside the rock.

"Don't get excited too early. Even more squares could be attached to this one. Then I have to restart once more."

But luck was on his side. The pyrite had exactly the size as his dent. He just had to remove the residuals and then he would be able to bring his gem to life. He scraped and cleaned the stone. And finally, the time had come. Four cuboids lay right in front of him. They matched each other and glowed the same dark-grey. He picked the gems up very slowly with his sore claws and inserted them into his dent. A strong tingling jolted through his body. He had brought his stone to life.

Rocket spent a few more sunrises on the island before he decided to visit the place of his childhood. Afterwards he wanted to set off again to explore the world.

He surged into the atmosphere. His destination was Lake Emerald where he wanted to take a bath. When he cut through the clouds, he noticed a group of pink dragons. A giant red dragon led the group around the rock which stretched far into The Huge Water.

"I think I will have a closer look."

CHARC

Foaming with rage The Red turned away in a flurry and retreated from his companions. Besides losing three stones, the bloody wimp knew his hiding place. Now he had to find a new one.

"I am going to make the whole clan suffer for this,"

he hissed in anger.

A gigantic bolt of red flames flashed from his mouth. He had to calm down. Firstly, he would return to his former retreat to fetch his Pink Brigade. While hurtling back he would ponder over the appropriate location for a new hide-out. He desperately needed two more bloodstones. The strategically best point would be close to Adama's Territory. Thus all the young dragons would pass him, no matter from which directions they came from. And were right in his line of vision. The danger of being found would of course be much higher as if he had a hiding place in the dense undergrowth. But he was willing to take the risk. He just needed a location with an unobstructed view to Adama's cliff.

His immense greed for revenge made him forget his usual, so helpful, precaution.

"I am going to punish all of them! I've time."

Charc collected his companions and headed to the Oracle.

One of the Pink dared to point out,

"That is a rather dangerous direction."

"Shut up. I know what I am doing,"

The Red grunted.

No objections were raised any more as none of them wanted to experience Charc's rage.

As soon as they got close to Adama's Territory The Red veered to the north. His destination was the land edging The Huge Water. He knew an estuary which cut far into the continent and which was surrounded by imposing mountains. This was the place where he wanted to have his second retreat. He would post a guard at the northernmost point of the continent so that he could be informed about each young dragon heading towards the Oracle.

Charc turned to his Pink Companions,

"That's the perfect hideout. Nobody will be able to find us here."

But none of them noticed the speck, that moved rocket-like, in the dusky sky which had already kept a keen eye on them for quite some time.

DRACO

Draco had arrived at Adama's.
"Draco, my friend. Your ways often lead to
me. But listen what I've to tell you:

Not the smallest scale of my skin
has to be wasted
The Blood of the Earth
will be able to revive your son

It's an erroneous belief
that the Black is as hard as the White
Radiancies of each and every element
are necessary
in order to boost the burst of the coal

If the six predetermined dragons
are at the right location at the right time
success will be guaranteed
You have to have patience to achieve
this

The Long-Desired has arrived
and is going to support you
with his ability to bundle and disperse

With a scale of mine you'll enhance your
forces
and obtain new ones
The Warrior stands ready
The Zircon, who will provide you with the
invisible rays,
you are going to find at the Council of the
Seven Stones
The Black Pearl will be able to inform you
about the time and the location
The one, who is capable to turn the sun
will act as a decoy
in order to lead you to victory
Hurry to the Council of the Seven Stones
to find the means to defeat The Red"

Exhausted by the long prophecy the
Oracle finished its speech. Adama
removed one of its golden scales from its
chest, warmed it up with a light jet of fire
and bent it so that it had the shape of an
open oval and put it around Draco's
emerald. A vigorous tingling jolted through
his body. Adama vanished and Draco was
allowed to leave.
Draco had a lot on his mind.
He would fly to the Council of the Seven
Stones to deliver his message.

"But before I do that, I will visit my family. Their cave is on my way."

Flying, Draco pondered Adama's actions and words thoroughly.

"Why did Adama put a gold ring around my protective stone? Why was the jolt so much stronger than the one which I had experienced when I got my dent for the entire stone? What was the Blood of the Earth? Who is the Black that isn't as hard as the White? Which elements were meant? Who were the six dragons? When was the appropriate time? Where was the correct location? But I guess, I know who the warrior is. I also know who possesses a zircon in the Council of the Seven Stones. And Nero has a black pearl. But is he really the one? Neither do I know who is capable to turn the sun."

Draco's head was spinning.

After numerous sunrises he arrived at Stella's cave. The situation appeared essentially unchanged, Sandy still kept a look over Sparkle while Stella tried everything to nurse him back to health. With her gentleness and her sunny disposition Bernadette had created a tranquil atmosphere in the den. Rocket and Rubi had left to look for their gems. The news, Draco broke to Stella, soothed her feelings. Even though she didn't know anything about the Blood of the Earth either. But if it was able to cure Sparkle that would be enough for her to know. Draco stayed another sunrise before he continued his way to the Assembly Place. The Council of the Seven Stones were still holding their meeting.

ROCKET

Rocket had observed The Red and his Pink Brigade for a few sunrises. He came to the conclusion that he had obviously discovered the brigade's new hide-out. At the moment it didn't make any sense to stay any longer.

"I've to get to the Council of the Seven Stones so that I can inform them what the Oracle's had predicted me. I am The Long-Desired, whatever that's supposed to mean? To be a wanderer between the worlds sounds cool. To find hidden memories, how interesting! I'm curious, when I'll use all that."

Rocket had found out that with the help of his stones, he was able to perceive, not only visible light, which was normal for him, but also two more ranges of wavelengths beyond the visible light. One wavelength was shorter, the other one was longer. He was capable of using these forms individually as well as in combination. It had taken him a long time until he could make the most out of these skills. But now it had many advantages. He was able to see through the clouds, to recognize obstacles far before he arrived there. Only the usage and the handling of the fourth cuboid was still unknown to him.

In the blink of an eye, Rocket got to the Assembly Place. Hakana, the representative of the desert, was the first one he met.

"I am Rocket, Draco's son. The Oracle predicted me that I am The Long-Desired. Here I am."

Hakana couldn't suppress a smile. He reminded her so much of his father, even though he wouldn't believe it.

"Well, well. The Long-Desired. Then come with me."

A strange feeling came over Rocket when Hakana looked at him. He had the impression as if one of his cuboids was sending a tingling through his body. He was convinced that it had been the cuboid, with which he was able to send and receive high frequency radiation.

"I'm just making it up."

On their way to the Assembly Place they met two other council members. Chockop, who presented the dragons of the air and Hinto, the dragon of the ocean. Both of them looked astonished when Hakana explained the situation. Yas, the dragon of the ice deserts and Adahy, the dragon-woman of the jungle were quickly called to join them. As soon as they arrived at the Council, they all settled down in their places. It was Hinto's turn to chair the meeting. This position rotated at regular intervals.

"Dear dragons, who represent the nation of this world, a long-desired event has taken place today. The Oracle has finally sent us the Council's missing member. Now we are complete. Adama has informed me that Draco will be here very shortly. He has received several information how we can defeat The Red. I suggest waiting for Draco's arrival and then we will continue our consultation. Gathering adjourned!"

Even though, Hinto had finished the official session, Rocket had to answer many curious questions.

It took Draco only a few sunrises before he arrived at the Assembly Place. Each representative had taken its place. So, had Rocket. Draco looked surprised when he noticed his son among the representatives.

"Rocket what are you doing here? Don't tell me that you are The Long-Desired?!"

"Yes dad, the Oracle has chosen me. I'm supposed to support the Council with magic, fire and electric conductivity."

Hinto interrupted their conversation.

"We are going to talk about this in peace and quiet. But first I'd like to hear from you, Draco, what the Oracle's predictions were."

Draco informed them about Adama's prophecy. While talking, a few things became clearer to him. Firstly, it was obvious now that Rocket, Diane, Hakana, Nero and himself were the ones who had to combat against The Red. Secondly, the one who was capable to turn the sun was the only one still missing. And at last, this was the place and time to find a way how to defeat The Red.

Draco turned to his son,

"Rocket do you possess any skills to bundle and disperse?"

"Yes, I can see things in the visible spectrum of light and also outside of it. Three of my cylinders enable me to do so. I can disperse and bundle the light. Just as I like it. But I haven't found out yet what I can do with my fourth cylinder."

"We'll find that out together,"

Hinto butted into Draco and Rocket's conversation.

"We have to call Nero and Diane to join us as soon as possible in order to find out who the dragon is that can turn the sun."

Rocket had suddenly an idea.

"I can remember a story aunt Bernadette told us when we were little. That might give us a clue."

"Yes Rocket, go ahead. We have to follow each and every trace."

And so, Rocket started to tell the story,

"Night had fallen. We had just crouched in the den, Nero lay a bit aloof from the rest of us when we demanded our regular good-night story. Aunt Bernadette asked us which story we wanted to listen to. I suggested my favorite story. It was about the dragon that couldn't only spit fire, but also light.

Aunt Bernadette started to tell the narration.

"Before your great-grand fathers were born, and even before their great-grand fathers, when the dragons had already started to fight each other on the other planet, there was an outstanding dragon by the name of Benisho, the Shining Light. Of course, he was able to spit fire but with the help of his protective stone he could also capture sunlight, bundle it in his stone and disperse it again 1000 times the original. Unfortunately, it isn't known which gem Benisho possessed. Neither do we know, how he was able to transform the sunlight into one deadly ray. At the beginning he was reluctant to use it. But when it turned out that his group was about to be defeated by the enemy, he felt eventually forced to attack them with the help of this deadly weapon for their own survival. The situation turned around and his group gained mastery. They slaughtered all dragons that belonged to the opponents. At this time Berhane and Erwaen had already left the planet.

"Is that the reason why we have the rule which forbids us to kill any dragon?"

Nero was always the first one to fire questions at aunt Bernadette.

"From where do we know all that when Berhane and Erwaen had already left?" Rubi objected.

"On this earth there is one dragon that holds the spirit of the universe; always has, always does and always will."

This provoked a soft murmur among us kids. Sparkle dared to speak,

"That is the Oracle, isn't it, Aunt Bernie?"
And again, the story which was supposed to lull us to sleep had the opposite effect. We were wide awake."

The entire Council was engrossed in pondering silence.

"In our oceans the descendants of Behane and Erwaen tell a similar story. You have to know, that not only these inhabit the oceans. There are also native dragons that had lived here before our ancestors arrived. And then there is a mixture of the two of course," explained Hinto.

"Now we know that it is possible to release a stream of light with the help of our stones. But we don't know how it can be done," remarked Hakana and looked around.

Again, Rocket's forehead tingled. Draco responded,

"Well, Adama mentioned the "Warrior" in her prophecy. I guess it is the dragon-girl, Diane. The one who got kidnapped, together with my son Sparkle, by The Red. Nero was able to rescue her. And when we released Sparkle out of Charc's claws she shot a stream of bundled flashes at him. I've forgotten that in the heat of the moment. But now I remember it clearly."

"Then it is possible that Nero wasn't just joking when he called her the Warrior Maid but that she really is the one the Oracle meant," gave Yas to think about.

"Nero and Diane were supposed to be brought to the Council anyway as we are convinced that the Oracle meant Nero when talking of the Black Pearl. And Diane is the Warrior. Draco do you know where they are right now?"

"Not exactly. All I know is that they wanted to fly to Stella's mother to fetch some dragon-skin powder for Sparkle."

"Well, in that case would you please make sure, that both of them get to the Assembly Place as soon as possible,"

and turning to Hakana he said,

"You try to figure out who the dragon is that can turn the sun."

The Assembly was closed.

"Draco, allow me to congratulate you on your kids. A world-wanderer who is born only every hundred thousand rotations and a water-dragon. Nero who possesses the black pearl cannot be anything else but the Black Pearl. An outstanding dragon like that is only born every ten thousand rotations. And all that from just one clutch of eggs,"

Yas, the dragon of the Icy Land, patted him appreciative on the back.

"Well, these were not only my genes. Half of it comes from Stella", Draco pointed out.

"You have never told us who your parents were, Draco."

"Well, ..."

Rocket joined in.

"Dad, may I accompany you?"

"I don't see any reason why you shouldn't?"

RUBI

Rubi took the shortest way to her mother's den. On her way she believed to have seen a dragon, perched high up on a cliff, which jutted far out into The Huge Water.

"Adama, I am already suffering from hallucinations. It's about time that I arrived." Fortunately, she was almost home, just one more sunrise and one more sunset lay ahead. Stella and Bernadette gave her a warm and hearty welcome when she arrived.

"Rubi, what made you come home? As I can see, you have found your stone. It is a beautiful gem. It's constantly glinting and twinkling in dark-red. But it is actually more a bowl than a stone, isn't it? How unusual." Her mother examined it very carefully. Bernadette added,

"A ruby-red bowl."

"Yes Mum, Aunt Berni, that's correct. What about Sparkle? Does he feel any better?" Stella answered sadly,

"Unfortunately, not. Sandy is staying with him. His wounds have healed but a scar has left. We treat it with dragon-skin powder to reduce its appearance and to soften and smoothen it. But he just doesn't come out of the coma."

"That's why I am here. The Oracle told me the following:

You are the blood of the earth
emerged from the interior
millions of rotations ago
born to heal
you are going to find your divine purpose

I thought, I'll come here. Maybe I can help Sparkle."

"Oh Adama, if that worked, I'd be the happiest dragon-mum in the world."

She felt a small glimmer of hope emerging inside her. The three of them went inside the cave. They found Sparkle lying unconscious, and Sandy looking after him.

"Hello Sandy."

"Hello Rubi."

"How is he?"

"Unchanged. He had been slipping in and out of coma for the past rotations but he isn't fully conscious, yet. Sometimes he rallies from the coma for a very short period but it looks as if he doesn't want to wake up."

"I came to help you. Maybe together we will be successful."

Rubi sat down in a comfortable upright position, her meditation posture. She quieted her mind as best as she could. Visions passed her inner eye, revealing Sparkle happily bathing, with his siblings, in Lake Emerald, enjoying himself intensively. Then she saw him at The Great Gathering indulging himself in dried fish; the food everybody else disliked so much, apart from Nero. She saw pictures showing Sparkle leaving for The Cold Land to find his new habitat.

Slowly, Rubi opened her eyes again. Stella, Bernadette and Sandy looked at her intently.

"Rubi, your bowl is filled with some liquid," Sandy noticed in great surprise.

"I assume Sparkle should take several gulps of it."

Stella fetched a leaf in order to collect the elixir which she then dropped into her son's mouth. This medicine didn't show an immediate effect. But all of them were convinced that this was the remedy to cure Sparkle. It didn't take long and the first achievements were noticeable. He became responsive for a longer period of time. Of course, they couldn't tell what was going on inside him. But then one sunrise he remarked to everyone's delight,

"I am absolutely starving. Why isn't anyone getting any food?"

That was the moment when Stella knew that her son was finally on his way to recovery.

As soon as Sparkle was on the mend, Sandy exempted herself from the self-imposed duty to look after him. She took off immediately and hurried back to Adama, to get her prophecy. Carefully, she approached the cliff. She felt slightly uncomfortable.

"And if the Oracle sends me away a second time? Then I will join the Pinks Brigade for good. No, of course, I won't. I hope I will never see these dumb brutes again."

When she arrived on the platform she peered slowly around. She couldn't see anyone. But a reassuring voice behind her was evidence enough that the Oracle was present.

"Your time has come
You offered your apologies
which makes past mistakes forgotten"

Sandy was most delighted. She burst with joy and listened eagerly to what Adama told her.

"You are able to turn the sun
that means, to reverse destiny
You embody nature with the veins of the earth
You are going to find your gem not far away from your mother's cave
in the south of the dense jungle
Your purpose is to support the dragons of the deserts
But be on guard against the Ghosts of the Past
they might be dangerous for you"

Sandy was overjoyed when the Oracle pressed the tip of a scale on her forehead. She thanked Adama profusely and then soared straight into the sky.

"I wonder what the Oracle meant by 'the Ghosts of the Past'? I won't pilfer any dragon-skin powder anymore. And neither will I swallow it."

But the Ghosts of the Past were already looking for young dragons, leaving Adama's rock.

NERO AND DIANE

Nero and Diane were on their way back from Raiffa's Finger to Stella's cave. Nero's grandmother had given them many different mixtures, made of ground dragon-skin powder. She had also instructed them, how to apply these. Heavily packed they traversed the estuary which divided the northern continent from the southern continent. They flew southwest across The Green Canopy. When they reached the coast, they wanted to turn south before veering eastwards again into the interior of the country. They had just arrived at the shore when a horrific scene of destruction came into their sight. It started at the banks and stretched far into the heart of the country.

"What has happened here?"

Shaken, Diane turned to Nero.

"I've no idea. And what's that?"

Nero pointed at a dragon which was barely able to stay in the air while flying.

"It won't take long and it'll plunge down."

"Diane, that is my sister Silent Wings!" exclaimed Nero. Dread filled his heart.

"Oh Adama, what has happened to her?"

They hurtled towards Silent Wings. Just in time to prevent her from sinking down.

"Silly, what's the matter with you?"

"Not now. I'm completely exhausted," she whimpered.

Nero supported her right wing with his left wing which made her wince. Diane did the same to support Silly's left flank. Nero noticed that his sister had found her stone. But apart from that she looked rather battered.

"If we continue flying sunrise and sunset we'll be at Mom's den in two sunrises. Come on, hurry up."

Carefully they landed in front of the hiding place. Stella and Bernadette came rushing outside instantaneously.

"Nero, Diane you are back? Oh Adama, what has happened to Silly?"

"We don't know. We found her in the south of the Isle of the Damned."

"Well then, come in."

Nero and Diane helped Silent Wings into the cave.

"Sparkle you are awake!"

Nero hurried to his brother.

"You've become a bit skinny. Rubi, you are here, too."

Rubi answered,

"And I guess that is really good. We can nurse Silly's injuries."

With united forces and the different dragon-skin powders from Grandmother Raiffa, they were able to heal Silly's wounds.

"By the way, where is Sandy?"

Stella explained to Nero that Sandy had left, to receive the Oracle's prophecies after Sparkle had started to recover.

DRACO AND ROCKET

It didn't take Draco and Rocket long to get to Stella's den.

"Is anyone hurt?"

Stella came rushing out of the cave, starring at them in alarm.

Draco and Rocket looked at each other in surprise.

"No, why?"

"Well, I have had a few wounds to treat recently. Therefore, I immediately think someone must be injured, as soon as anyone of you shows up. But what leads you to me?"

Draco explained Stella why they had returned.

"Well, then come in."

Draco glanced around the den.

Apart from Stella and Bernadette, he noticed that also Nero, Diane, Rubi, Silent Wings and Sparkle were present. As Rocket had arrived with him there was only one of his children missing, Sandy.

"Sparkle, I'm so glad to see that you are conscious and already enjoying food again."

"I don't know what you are all talking about. I am not that voracious."

"It looks as if we are having a family reunion. But unfortunately, I have a task to fulfil. The Council asked me to get Nero and Diane to the Assembly Place. Where is Sandy, by the way?"

"Sandy is on her way to the Oracle to obtain her prophecy," Stella informed him. Rocket suddenly felt uneasy.

"Dad, I saw a dragon of the Pink Brigade observing The Huge Water. He was sitting on the rock which juts far out into the ocean. I also saw The Red staying there. I assumed that this must be Charc's new hide-out. It is a location from where you can easily spot all the young dragons skimming across the continent in order to get to the Oracle."

"Then I was right. I also saw a dragon. perching on that rock, when I was flying back home," Rubi added.

"I think we should support Sandy. She mustn't get caught again by The Red." Draco looked around.

"Who will come with me?"

Everyone was willing to join him. Draco decided to let Rocket, Nero and Diane accompany him.

"Don't worry. We will be Sandy's invisible guardians."

Stella and Bernadette exchanged meaningful glances.

"Hopefully, all goes well."

HAKANA

"The one who is capable to turn the sun.

That cannot be meant literally. No dragon could do that. It doesn't matter how strong and powerful he or she is,"
Hakana kept brooding.
But what was it, the Oracle wanted to express?
"I've to go through all the ancient myths to find a clue. And maybe it could be helpful to visit the oldest dragons our world. I'm going to consult The Wise dragons that are most respected by our tribe."
Thus, Hakana set off for the Hakan Desert, after which she was named. She was extremely delighted to traverse the foothills of the mountains, to reach the prairie and the savannah with its sparse vegetation and finally to catch sight of the vast area of sand dunes. Each dune looked different. The various wind directions and the different air currents had shaped each dune individually. She thought to herself,
"There is no big difference between the ocean and the dunes. One is water, the other is sand. A blustery wind churns both

of them and can have dreadful consequences."

She loved the smell of hot dry air and the scorching sun on the horizon. Hakana perched on one of the dunes.

The members of her tribe lived in solitude as hermits, just as all the other dragons did. Only mothers and their hatchlings as well as old dragons and dragons in need, live in a community.

"I will visit the nearest oasis first. It is called Wadi Aijana, Eternal Blossom. I can ask Dichali, the talkative, for her advice."

Hakana swooped gracefully towards Wadi Aijana. It didn't take long and the little green island, surrounded by dunes, seemed to appear out of nowhere, in the desert.

"I just love it. My homeland is so beautiful." Hakana landed on the edge of the oasis. As soon as she had touched the ground, she felt as if being watched. She turned into exact that direction and spotted a huge chalcedony. Its light merged from light-blue to turquoise. This gem represents the elements of water and air, whereas air could also stand for exchange and communication. Then a green-blue dragon came into sight. Its entire body was covered by countless wrinkles.

"Well, if that isn't an old dragon?!"

Hakana introduced herself,

"My name is Hakana. I am from the Council of the Seven Stones...."

"I know you. My name is Dichali, the one who talks a lot. What makes you come to my oasis? Why are you here?"

Hakana explained the reason.

"Unfortunately, I know nothing about such a dragon you are looking for. Of course, I do know the narrations of our past. But I don't know more than you already do. The only one I could recommend is The Chronicler, Kaga.

"Where does he live?"

"In a mountain cave located in the mountain range that is called The Invisible Summits. You have to cross the southern continent first, then you skim The Huge Water until you reach a cluster of islands. It is called The Telfis. After you've passed it, Chendris will appear quite soon. The Invisible Summits tower directly from the seabed and rise to many thousand dragon lengths."

"Thank you Dichali. I'll give it a try."

"Oh, why don't you stay a bit longer? We could have a pleasant conversation."

"I am terribly sorry. But my duty doesn't allow me to stay any longer. Thank you very much. Adama be with you."

"Adama be with you. Good luck, Hakana." Hakana spread her mighty wings again and took off.

Muttering to herself Dichali, disappeared under her palm trees,

"She could have taken a bit of time only for a short chat. Who knows when I will have a visitor again?"

Hakana had left the Eternal Blossom and veered northeast towards The Green Canopy. She crossed first the jungle and then The Huge Water before she broke her journey on one of the isles of The Telfis which rested just off the coast of Chendris. It was the same island where Rubi had taken a break. Hakana traversed an arm of water but landed at the coast in great astonishment. A massive mountain range towered along the coast. It lay mysterious and unexplored. The mountains seemed untamed and had no end in sight. Most impressive was the immense height. The mountain range lived literally up to its name, The Invisible Summits, as from a certain altitude onwards, the tips of the mountains were hidden behind clouds.

"I'll try to cut through the clouds and find the cave from above."

Hakana twisted up into the air. As soon as she got into the clouds she started to shiver in the icy temperatures and the cold dampness.

"Do I have to experience this? I am a desert dweller!"

She gritted her teeth and rose higher. The air became thinner and chillier which caused her additional problems. But suddenly she burst through the clouds. An amazing view opened up. Below her stretched a white cloud cover that extended as far as she could see, pierced by single snow-covered peaks, above that a brilliant blue sky. The air was crisp and perfectly clear. Hakana, taken by complete surprise, almost forgot to breathe.

"I wonder, whether I could walk on it."

She tried to perch, but immediately sank into the cold damp cloud.

"It is freezing. I'd rather gain altitude again. I am sure that Kaga's cave is located somewhere in this frostiness."

Hakana soared even higher and circled a few times in the air.

Slowly she realized, that she would never find him from above.

"I obviously have to look for him in the bitter cold."

Hakana was just about to break through the clouds again when she suddenly spotted a fast-moving speck hovering in the distance.

"I'll ask whether Kaga is known here in this area and where I could find him."

Shortly after, she was at the other dragon's side.

"Adama be with you. I'm Hakana. A member of the Council of the Seven Stones...."

"Adama be with you. I know you Hakana. What's your reason for coming here? You are far away from the Council of the Seven Stones."

"I'm searching Kaga, The Chronicler. Do you know where he lives?"

"Yes, that might be possible."

"What do you mean? Come on, either you know him, or you don't. Do you?"

Hakana was about to lose her temper.

"Wow, take it easy, Daughter of the Desert. I am Kaga. Why have you come here?"

For the first time Hakana really looked at him. A massive three-piece mountain-crystal crowned his forehead. The largest piece was the one closest to his nostrils. The two other parts, which lay right behind the first one, were both a little bit smaller in size. His wrinkled skin, which shimmered in every color and shade of grey, were evidence of his advanced age. His friendly kind eyes watched her curiously. Hakana explained him why she had come to see him and that she was in need of his wisdom.

"I suggest flying to my shelter. Here, up in the air, it isn't very comfortable to have a conversation."

He turned around and Hakana followed him. His cave, which wasn't far away, was facing south. The warm sunrays penetrated far inside.

"Oh Adama, what's that!" she exclaimed in excitement.

She was surrounded by a constant shifting and shimmering of countless of jewels. The entire wall was covered with different gemstones.

"I am not only a chronicler but also the Guard of the Gemstones of the deceased dragons. For thousands of rotations the dragons have come to my place to find their final resting place. I keep their stones inside my walls for eternity. When I'd like to hear a story about one of the dragons, I have to tap the respective stone and it will tell me its narration. No one else has this gift. It is due to my crystals. One of the small crystals absorbs the information, the second one processes these and the third one, the big one, stores the information and transfers them to me."

"Could that also work with other stones and rays?"

"Quite possible."

"Do you also have Berhane's and Erwaen's stones?"

"Oh my dear, you know very well that these two left this world."

"Ah well, of course. And Adama is still alive. But what about our ancestors' second litter?"

"Their stones are here."

Kaga advanced further down into the cave and pointed at four gemstones.

"These are Chesmu's, Abebi's, Hodari's and Irie's jewels. Four dragons of the second litter."

"How amazing! Wait, may I guess which stone belonged to which dragon."

"If you want to do that, go ahead."

"Chesmu, the Brave, possessed the tourmaline. The moonstone belonged to Abebi, the Desired. Hodari, the Strong, owned the sodalite and Irie, the Beauty, owned the tiger eye. I am right, aren't I?" Expectantly, Hakana looked at Kaga.

"Well done! All of them were correct. But now let's focus on what has brought you to see me."

Kaga slowly strolled along the cave walls. Once and again he touched one of the stones, shook his head and continued walking. He stopped, turned around walked back but shook his head again.

"You said you are looking for a dragon that can turn the sun?"

"Yes, I am supposed to search for this dragon."

"Throughout our entire history there has never been a dragon which was capable of turning the sun."

Hakana was about to lose hope.

"But what I can tell you is the following. There are protective stones which can turn the paths of destiny with the support of their dragons. That might help you. But then you have to know what exactly the Oracle told the young dragon."

"In that case I've to find that very dragon."

"Good luck Hakana, Daughter of the Desert."

"I highly appreciate your help, Kaga, The Chronicler and Guard of the Gemstones.

Kaga, may I come back, after I have completed this task?

I am highly interested in these stones and the information they hold."

"We have to ask the Council. It is the Council that decides who is allowed to gain access to the gemstones. Only then the stones will reveal their secrets."

"Adama be with you, Kaga."

"Adama be with you, Hakana."

Hakana left the den, spread her wings and flew westwards above the clouds towards The Huge Water.

CHARC

"Master, Master, I've just seen a dragon hurtling to the Oracle! It looked just like the little one we had already captured once before!"

"Well, that is finally good news again. Return to your lookout and watch very carefully. Take a companion with you and send him back to me as soon as you know which direction the babe is taking."

"Yes, Master, we'll do as you say."

The Pink grabbed one of his fellows. Together they dashed to the viewpoint. Charc rejoiced silently.

"Adama always wants the best for me. If I get this little wimp, it will be the beginning of the brood's end."

This time The Red didn't share any of his ripe fruits. He had to be wide awake and absolutely focused. A few sunrises passed by but neither of them returned. Charc became increasingly impatient. In the end, he couldn't bear it any longer. He leapt up, hind legs digging into the ground, lunging forward powerfully towards the lookout.

"You idiots. You have missed her! I'd really love to cremate you right here and now.

Just look around. You can observe the entire area. How can you be so bloody stupid? What's inside your brain? Probably just pink fruits! I guess, I have to scare some sense into you. The little one has already left to find her gem and you have overlooked her. If the next young dragon approaches and you make the same mistake, there will be nothing left of you but a small heap of ashes. Did you get it?"

"Yes, Master. Of course,"

they stammered defensively,

Charc left the two behind. While flying back to his hiding place he pondered,

"Why didn't they notice the little one? There is only one possibility, she must have turned south immediately. Nonsense! There is only water. Well, wherever this bloody bitch is, this gem is obviously lost again. I desperately need an additional stone as soon as possible."

SANDY

Sandy was on her way to the southern edge of The Green Canopy. She was so relieved that she had received her prophecy and that she didn't have to cross half of Muraco.

At the time, when Charc had still been sure of his victory, Draco, Rocket, Nero and Diane were already flying to Lake Emerald. They had decided to seek a hiding place which provided sufficient distance to the Oracle. It was Rocket's task to survey the happenings since he was by far the fastest one of them. His low frequency cylinder enabled him to observe the Pink Brigade through the clouds without being detected. He was prepared to wait for a long time. But very soon he already caught sight of a dragon heading directly from Adama's rock towards Charc's ambush site. In an instant Rocket dashed forward using his rocket propulsion. His head-protection flapped down in front of his face. In next to no time he was by the dragon's side. It was Sandy. He fell back into his gliding modus and she gazed at him in great surprise,

"Rocket, what are you doing here?"
"I've been looking for you. The Red is searching you. He has a new hideout. And if you had continued flying into that direction you would have fallen right into his clutches."
"Oh, Adama!"
"Indeed. What did the Oracle tell you? In which direction are you supposed to fly in order to find your stone?"

"You embody nature with the veins of the earth
You are going to find your gem not far away from your mother's cave
In the south of the dense jungle
Your purpose is to support the dragons of the deserts"

"Well, then we will avoid that direction. Let's change your course. We won't target your destination directly. Let's take a circuitious route. Daddy and the others are waiting for us to escort you. They are at Lake Emerald."
"Is it that bad?"
"Yep, I think this bastard stops at nothing."
Thus, Sandy and Rocket took a course more to the south. In order to stay

unnoticed, they flew continuously above the clouds. Finally, they reached Lake Emerald unscathed. From there all of them hurtled immediately towards Sandy's destination. And again, they stayed permanently above the protective cloud cover while making their way past Stella's den to the north, towards the edge of The Green Canopy. Sandy took the lead. The others only accompanied her. The search for one's gemstone was a task that each dragon had to undertake on their own.

STELLA AND BERNADETTE

"It has become pretty quiet here since everybody has left."
Once Sparkle's strength had returned, he had become more and more restless with each additional sunrise. Staying at his mother's cave had boosted his boredom and had damped his spirits. Therefore, he had decided to set off to find his new habitat. Only a small scar, inflicted by Charc, was left behind next to his opal. With the help of Rubi's drink, he had even overcome the mental pain. Rubi herself had also departed in order to help wherever she was needed. Silent Wings had been the last one to leave. She knew that she was supposed to fulfil her purpose too. Her plumage radiated again in its former splendor and her injured right wing had healed.
"I am going to be a wanderer in the service of the dragons. Whatever the Oracle meant by that, I'll find it out."
Thus, the two sisters were left on their own in the cave.
"Let's go on an excursion to Lake Emerald, shall we? We always had such a good time

with the kids there. We'll go hunting, bathe in the lake and then we'll return."

"Great idea!" Bernadette agreed.

They satisfied their hunger with some springbucks which lived in the savannah edging the lake. Shortly before darkness fell, they reached the southernmost part of the lake. A waterfall cascaded down the steep cliffs.

"Tomorrow we'll take a long bath."

The sun rose slowly in the east and glittered on the turquoise-green mountain lake. Stella and Bernadette looked for a shallow spot in the crystal-clear water. They behaved like kids splashing in the lake. They were happily dabbling and diving, spluttering and spitting in the knee-deep water, when suddenly a shadow darkened their cheerful time. Charc alighted with two of his companions on the shore right behind Bernadette. Stella froze. Her heart jumped then she exclaimed in alarm,

"Bernie, Bernie, there….!"

"What's the matter?"

Bernadette whirled around in a flurry. Mortal fear clenched her heart for a moment but then she commanded,

"Stella, get out of here!"

"No!" Stella stood powerless to do anything.

"In the name of your kids! I'll distract him and you try to get out of here!"

"Well, ladies,"

Charc sneered,

"what a pleasant surprise in the early morning. Isn't that a stroke of luck? Bernie, it's lovely to see you again. And now I kindly ask the ladies to accompany us."

"Stella, now!"

Bernadette shot a tremendous stream of fire at the three baffled looking opponents. This was Stella's chance, as Charc and his companionons turned their heads towards the fire instead, giving Stella time to get away. She lunged powerfully out of the water and spiraled herself up high into the air where she finally disappeared.

A second jet of fire, spitted by Bernadette, obscured Charc's vision. He couldn't see in which direction Stella was vanishing. That was too much for him. Hate crossed his face,

"Get her! Surely the three of us will manage to overpower one single dragon-lady!"

He advanced towards Bernadette who immediately edged away. She surpassed herself, defending herself using fire, claws and tail. But in the end, she had to give up.

"Now, baby, I want you to submit yourself to my fellows. They haven't had fun in a long time."

Charc and the Pinks tied her up with lianas. She tried to wrench herself away but to no avail. They even gagged her before dragging her to their new hideout.

"The boss said, she is ours."

Curious they formed a menacing half-circle around her. With their dirty, pink claws they poked her body when The Red showed up again.

"Sorry guys, I've changed my mind. She is mine. I am going to beget many little dragons who can then lead me directly to their gemstones. As Daddy isn't evil. Daddy wouldn't harm a fly! Heh-heh!"

Charc was so delighted about his new fantastic idea that he didn't notice the faint but dissatisfied mumbling among his mates.

SANDY

Sandy followed by Draco, Rocket, Nero and Diane had reached the edge of The Green Canopy.

"Sandy, this task only you can fulfil. You have to do it on your own. But Rocket will keep a keen eye on you from above. The rest of us will stay down here and wait for you to return or to support you in case of an emergency,"

Draco explained his daughter.

Rocket soared up into the air while Sandy took off heading towards the jungle. Shortly after Rocket had switched back into the mode of leisurely drifting, he noticed something rather peculiar. With his eyes he saw The Green Canopy. A broad blue snake winded through the impenetrable jungle. Several minor creeks flowed into this major stream which finally joined the ocean somewhere in the far distance. But with the help of one of his protective stones he was able to penetrate The Green Canopy and to "look' below the surface of the earth. Rocket was aware of the fact that down there a large quartz deposit lay hidden, not even very deep, inside the ground.

"How could I inform Sandy about it? Of course, she has to find her gem on her own. But until now she has only been searching for her stone in the wrong direction."

Nervously, Rocket circled far overhead.

"I'll let Daddy know. He might know what to do."

Rocket returned to the others and explained Draco the situation.

"Daddy, if she keeps searching there, where she has been looking, she will never find her stone. I've discovered a vast deposit. She would only have to pick one. But we aren't allowed to help her, are we?"

"Well to be exact, it is said that each young dragon has to fly to the Oracle on its own and then seek the stone. But I've never heard that you aren't allowed to provide assistance. Even your mother had some support."

"Really?"

"Yes, and I think we should tell Sandy where she should continue searching."

Draco and Rocket gave Sandy directions where to find the quartz deposit. But even with the knowledge, where to look for her stone, it was hard work for her to get to the site. She had to cut through the dense jungle and when she eventually arrived exhausted at the right spot she had to laboriously dug for her stone. But finally, she found what she had been searching for. A dark-green pyramid with thin veins of red gleamed at her. She cleaned it meticulously from mud and dirt. It still seemed dull and shadowed. She inserted the heliotrope happily into her mark. A strong tingling jolted through her body. Sandy had found her protective stone. It was alive and radiated brightly towards her family.

"Oh Adama, that is a fantastic stone!" Nero said admiringly.

When Sandy turned towards Rocket, he winced and exclaimed,

"Sandy, what are you doing?"

"What do you mean?"

"You can't bombard me with your rays!"

"I didn't do anything."

"Daddy, didn't you notice it?"

They tried to figure out who of them was sensitive to Sandy's rays and who wasn't.

Rocket, who had been able to see the quartz deposit with the help of his cylinder, was also capable to perceive Sandy's rays.

"Do you think you could send me a strong intensive beam instead of these weak rays? Go ahead and try."

Sandy focused intensely on bundling the energy. Nothing was to be seen. Only Rocket suddenly sat on his bottom looking completely puzzled. He had been thrown off balance.

"Are you crazy?" he gasped.

"You said, I should try!"

Rocket grunted, "Yeah, right. That's what I've said."

"If I can do it, then you should be able to do it, too. We don't have to wipe each other out. You can choose a different target."

"Good, let's go for it."

Sandy channeled the energy once more and sent a cascade of rays towards Rocket. This time he was prepared to receive them. He collected them and shot them off again. But he got pushed off balance and landed on his bottom one more time. The recoil of his own beams had given him such a severe blow that he got knocked over.

"Oh Adama! That is the effect of my fourth cylinder. I am capable to catch rays, amplify these and emit them."

Only now he noticed that he had set a tree on fire with his bundled power.

"That was me. Wow! I cannot believe it! Have I actually done that?"

"Are you aware of the fact that we've just made a major step? Sandy, please do that again with Diane and Nero, but less intense. When you practice it with me you can use all your strength."

Diane was the one who performed the task most accurately. With the arrow's shaft of her stone she caught Sandy's beams and then aligned her arrowhead with her target. She aimed at her goal with perfect precision.

Draco used the gold ring, which framed his emerald, in order to catch Sandy's rays. He bundled these in his stone where they caused a flash of light. It released itself out of the middle and illuminated their surroundings.

Nero on the other hand, could neither sense the rays nor bundle them, let alone shooting them off.

"Why me again? It's always me. Why is it me again who cannot do it?!"

Grumbling he withdrew himself from the others. Draco followed him.

"Nero, the Oracle predicted that you would also be one of the dragons who will defeat The Red. Be patient. You have other, different skills which we will definitely need."

Although Nero was still muttering a string of curses, Draco's words had a soothing effect on his mind.

STELLA

Stella had forsaken her hiding. Under the protection of Bernie's fire stream, she had been darting up into the air. Without further thinking she had hidden behind the thundering waterfall. And to be on the safe side she had crawled even further into one of the damp dens, where she had crouched for several sunrises, before she dared to emerge again. Nobody was to be seen, neither The Red with his companions nor Bernadette. Stella was very careful to stay unnoticed, as they could have hidden somewhere nearby.

"What shall I do? Should I try to find The Red in order to find Bernadette? Rocket had mentioned a location. No, that would be utter suicide. Maybe I should head home. No, that doesn't make sense either. Everybody has left the den. Oh Adama, what am I supposed to do? What can I do to help my sister?"

Contrary to all hopes Stella started for home. Half way back she encountered a gliding dragon. The light-blue wings were barely distinguishable from the azure-blue of the sky.

"Silly, what are you doing here?"
"Mum, you know what the Oracle told me.

You will become a wanderer
in the service of the dragons

I always get guided to dragons who require my help. And right now, it is obviously you, who needs me most."
"Indeed. That's absolutely true. But I'm convinced that Aunt Bernadette is in dire straits, too."
"What has happened?"
Stella told Silent Wings Bernadette's devastating situation.
"I don't think he dared to kill her. But I don't want to think about what he and his fellows might do to her."
"Mum, we will find a solution."

Bernadette was immediately convinced, that Charc knew that his forced copulation had been a success.
"What shall I do? If I tell him, that I haven't conceived, he will rape me over and over again. He won't stop until he finally believes that his sperm has found its counterpart in my belly and has fertilizes an egg cell. But if I tell him that he was

successful, he won't let me out of his sight just to prevent me from fooling him. In any case, it will give me enough time to think how I could escape. And when the little ones have hatched, there will still be plenty of rotations before they can fly to the Oracle let alone, finding their gems. And then I will get a last and final opportunity to flee, as he can't accompany all of them at the same time to the Oracle."

Reluctantly she informed The Red about his "success".

"That is wonderful! You see, we are the perfect match. Now I have to make sure that you won't lack anything. As only strong dragons get powerful stones. Don't you dare swallow any herbs in order to lose your eggs. Your bodyguards will constantly observe you before and after sunrise."

Bernadette suppressed her distaste and reminded him,

"I've to look for a nesting spot."

"But baby, we already have our sweet home,"

Charc chuckled with an evil grin.

"If you mean that place where you kidnapped our kids and where I buried them in the end, you can definitely forget that!"

Rage was boiling in Bernadette's voice.

"Well, you don't have a choice. We won't spend any time looking for another place. I know, this is what you are hoping for. You believe to be discovered and rescued by one of your dragon-friends. No, no, baby, we are returning to our sweet home and you will pretend living the happy family life until I pick up the kids for an adventure trip. Did you get that?"

Right now, Bernadette knew well, that her only option was to give in.

"Of course."

"See baby, we can agree so easily. You do what I want and we will live very peacefully together."

Bernadette thought,

"I doubt this. I still have so much time left. And there will be an opportunity for me to escape. I won't bring up my second litter in that cave of great misfortune. First of all, the cave has collapsed and secondly it is the grave of my offspring. Even though, these hatchlings were conceived in misery they still have the right to spend a carefree childhood; without you. I'll take care of that. Even if it takes my life."

"But now you have to excuse me, baby. My fellows have just informed me about a young dragon heading to the Oracle's. I'm sure you will understand that I cannot miss that. Your bodyguards will take good care of you."

Bernadette struggled with all her might to get free and tried to spit fire at the same time.

"Gag her again. You are so stupid, you'd let yourselves get incinerated."

In his immeasurable greed for the gems The Red seemed to have forgotten his usual safety precautions. He followed his victim all the way to the Oracle.

THE COUNCIL OF THE SEVEN STONES

As soon as Draco, Rocket, Nero, Diane and Sandy finished practicing, they set off for the Nekan Desert, where the Council of the Seven Stones would be meeting. It was the same place where The Great Gathering took place every two hundred rotations. They skimmed over The Green Canopy and traversed the estuary close to Raiffa's Finger. When they reached the coast, they veered towards the north. After ten sunrises they alighted on the Assembly Place. Their meeting had been arranged for the following sunrise. Rocket felt very proud to be among the councilmembers.

"Now, I am one of them. I am the youngest member of the Council of the Seven Stones."

Hinto opened the meeting.

"Dear Council members, dear guests. I am pleased to welcome you. As I heard you have done fantastic work. But now I'll pass the word to you, Draco."

Draco informed the Council,

"It was pure coincidence that Rocket and I met Nero and Diane. When we arrived at

Stella's hideout they were still there. We found out that Sandy was on her way to the Oracle. Unfortunately, or thank Adama, The Red had changed his hiding place and now we know, where his ambush is located. He is staying right in the approach path which young dragons have to take, when flying to the Oracle. Rocket had accidentally discovered the ambush. We had decided to escort Sandy on her way finding her protective stone."

Hinto turned to Sandy,

"So, and you are Sandy, aren't you? But let's take one step at a time. Please Draco, carry on."

"As you can see Sandy was successful. We were still at the location where she had found her gem, when we noticed that Sandy was able to receive, amplify and emit rays. We practiced right there and found out that all of us are able to do that. Rocket is the strongest one of us when it comes to receiving and bundling beams. What the dosage is concerned that is actually something we still have to work on. Diane, on the other hand, works most precisely. With the help of my gold ring, which Adama once put around my emerald, I can also receive, bundle and

emit rays. It is a hot bolt of lightning which I can cast through the center of my gemstone."
Hinto rose to speak again,
"Well, let's sum up everything we know by going through the Oracle's prophecy once again, point by point.

It's an erroneous belief
that the black is as hard as the white

We still have to find out what exactly is meant by that.

Beams of each and every element are necessary
in order to boost the burst of the coal
If the six predetermined dragons
are at the right time at the right location
success will be guaranteed

Draco, Rocket, Hakana, Nero, Diane and Sandy are the dragons who have to make joint efforts in order to burst the coal. We still have to find out what is meant by coal.

The right time and the right location
will guarantee success

You'll have to have patience to achieve this. We will see about that later.

The Long-Desired has arrived
and will support you
with his ability to bundle and disperse

Rocket has impressively proofed that.

With a scale of mine you'll enhance your forces
and obtain new ones

This matter we can regard as settled.

The Warrior stands ready

Diane, are you ready?"
"Sure I am. But I'd like to say something. The Red is also capable of emitting bundled beams. When we were rescuing Sparkle, I saw The Red trying to remove Sparkle's gemstone with such a beam. It was very painful for Sparkle. Therefore, it is absolutely essential to find out which rays Charc is able to emit and how to combat it."
"That is an additional point which we'll have to verify.

The Zircon, who will provide you with the
invisible rays,
you are going to find at the Council of the
Seven Stones

Hakana that refers to you. Unfortunately, I
have to admit that I, personally, have
never noticed any rays."
Rocket became restless. As Hinto realized it
he turned to him,
"What's the matter young dragon?"
"I've noticed it. Each time she looks at me,
my head starts to prickle."
"As long as it doesn't prickle anywhere else,
it's okay."
Nero couldn't suppress this remark, which
caused common laughter.
"Let's stay focused, my friends."
Hinto cleared his throat for silence.

"The Black Pearl will be able to inform you
about the time and the location

Nero, that will be your part.

The one, who is capable to turn the sun
will act as a decoy
in order to lead you to victory

Hakana has been looking for the one who is capable to turn the sun."
Sandy shyly cleared her throat,
"Chairperson, may I tell you what the Oracle prophesied to me?"
"If it is relevant to this subject."
"I think it is.

Your time has come
You offered your apologies
which makes past mistakes forgotten
You are able to turn the sun
That means to reverse destiny
You embody nature with the veins of the earth
You are going to find your gem not far away from your mother's cave
In the south of the dense jungle
Your purpose is to support the dragons of the deserts
But be on guard against the ghosts of the past"

An audible gasp went around the council and among the guests. It was Draco who spoke first,
"Sandy, you are meant. You are able to turn the sun. We all took it literally. But it

means that you are able to turn destiny for the better."

"But Daddy, …."

"There is no but. The Oracle has determined you. You'll grow with your tasks."

Adahy, the representative of the jungle interfered,

"By the way, are you aware of the fact that four out of six chosen dragons come from Draco and his family?"

Hinto objected,

"I'd not doubt the Oracle's prophecy."

"I just thought if something goes amiss almost an entire family will be wiped out."

"We don't even want to think about that. Now let's talk about the last part of Adama's prophecy.

Hurry to the Council of the Seven Stones so that you can find the means to defeat The Red"

It was the first time that Yas spoke,

"I suggest practicing these skills which you have required by the means of your stones and rays. To me this seems to be most important now. I see this as our great chance. The information, Hakana has brought us, might be useful too. And then we have to think of a battle plan how to get The Red to the right location at the right time. It has to be immaculately planned. And with Nero's help we should be able to figure that out. This will put us in a good position to defeat Charc."

As they had reached general agreement Hinto declared the meeting closed.

"Mum, what do you think? Shall we return to our cave, get some dragon-skin powder and bring that to grandma Raiffa? The rest of the powder we will hide deep inside the den. And then we'll continue flying to the Council of the Seven Stones? I suppose Daddy and the others will be there. If not, the Council might at least know what has happened."

"That's a good idea. But I am rather concerned about Bernadette. Isn't there anything we could do to help her?"

"No Mum, we wouldn't stand a chance against him on our own. He would probably tear us to pieces. Furthermore, The Red might be long gone."

"You are right. Let's fly to grandma Raiffa." Before they left, Stella dug a hole at the rear of the den, where she had already once deposited her eggs. This time she buried half of her dragon-skin powder in that very corner. After digging she felt exhausted. Nevertheless, they departed immediately.

"Silly, please will you do me a favor? Don't mention what happened to Aunt

Bernadette and me when you are talking to grandma. It is already bad enough as it is. I don't want her to worry constantly about Bernadette. And that is exactly what she would do."

"That's okay, Mum. And maybe we will find The Red and Aunt Bernie soon."

"You are an eternal optimist."

After an exhausting flight, at least for Stella, they perched on Raiffa's Finger shortly after sunrise. It was a glorious morning. The sun had just risen. Spherical in shape it shed orange light while lifting itself out of the ocean. It would become a hot day for the dragons in this area.

As soon as they landed in front of Raiffa's cave, Stella's mother immediately padded towards them.

"Hello my dear kids! What a lovely surprise! What brings you to see me?"

Stella and Silent Wings exchanged a quick glance.

"Well, as all my hatchlings have left me I wanted to discover the world. On my way I accidentally met Silly. We decided to come and visit you,"

Stella answered her mother.

"What a wonderful idea. Well, then come in. Unfortunately, I can only offer you some fruits of the jungle. But please help yourselves."

"Thank you. That is just fine, Mum. Silly and I will go hunting for you so that you'll have some meat to store."

"That is so kind of you."

Stella and Silly decided to stay for a few sunrises. They handed over their dragon-skin powder to Raiffa. She already had an ample supply of it and now explained them the different compositions and mixtures. Stella promised to visit her again on her way back home. During that visit she would pick up some of the powder and take it with her. On one of these sunrises, they were just comfortably sitting in front of the den, when Raiffa asked,

"Stella, where is Bernadette, by the way?" she demanded.

"You were inseparable, weren't you? I am surprised she hasn't come with you."

Stella started to think frantically. Why hadn't she thought about this question ahead of time. What should she tell her mother? Now it was too late.

"Well Mum, Bernadette preferred to stay in the den. She said that she wasn't as keen on adventures as I am right now."

Raiffa was satisfied with that answer.

"Yes, she has always been calmer than you've been; less restless."

They swapped stories until Stella requested, "Mum, do you know by any chance where Bernadette raised her hatchlings?"

Raiffa flinched, she was immediately alarmed.

"Has Bernadette told you about her cruel fate?"

"Yes, why shouldn't she?"

"Because she locked it in her heart and never wanted to talk about it again. That's why. Now, tell me the truth, my dear. I might almost be unable to fly and I might be your mother who doesn't have to know everything, but in this case, I absolutely insist that you tell me the truth."

Stella hesitated, but she also realized that her mother had the right to know the truth. When Stella started to tell the story, Silly pricked her ears and listened most carefully once again.

"What an insane bastard! His mother should have drowned him."

Raiffa was outraged.

"You know his mother?"

"Yes, of course I do. And so, do you."

"I do? How come?" she asked puzzled.

"It is Gazalay, The Mysterious."

"But that is Draco's mother!"

"That is correct. Draco and Charc are half-siblings. Draco was already an adult when The Red was born. He was a problem child from his first day on. Each time when we met at The Great Gathering Gazalay told us of another misdeed. At that time, by the way, I was still able to fly long distances. Gazalay informed us that she would have been glad if he had found his gem. She longed for the moment that he'd finally have grown up. But when this moment eventually arrived things became even worse."

"And who is Charc's father?"

"She has never told me that."

"And who is Draco's father?"

"Ikechi, The Power Adama's."

Stella and Silent Wings stared at Raiffa open-mouthed, unable to speak.

HAKANA

Hakana rushed directly back to the Council of the Seven Stones.

"I will definitely return to Kaga and his cave, if the Council allows me to do that. I'd love to know how to read stones."

She crossed the land bridge which connected Chendris with the island Telfi, which rested just off the coast. She glided north of the narrow archipelago which was called Tyrania, skimmed over the ocean, passed Draco's cliff and finally got to the Assembly Place. The members of the Council were already awaiting her impatiently. Hinto began to speak.

"Well, Hakana, Daughter of the Desert, were you able to find out who the dragon is that can turn the sun?"

"Dear Hinto, President of the Council, unfortunately I have to inform you that I've returned without the answer."

She slowly shifted her gaze from one to another. Rocket felt another tingling running through his body. Sandy had noticed it and had to smile.

"I wonder where exactly he feels this tingling sensation,"

she thought to herself.

Hakana who had watched Sandy at that very moment mused,

"Who has a tingling sensation and where?"

"Well, Rocket, when he looks at you,"

Sandy answered mentally.

Both of them very completely baffled. They stopped for a moment. Hakana was the first who recomposed herself.

"You can read my thoughts! How do you do that?"

"You can also read my thoughts! How do you do that?"

"I guess, my stone can catch the beams of your stone. My brain processes these signals and with the help of my stone, the answer can be transferred to you."

"And this obviously also works the other way around."

"Ladies, could we please focus on our subject?"

Hinto had noticed that Hakana and Sandy were staring at each other. He interrupted them without realizing the importance of the matter.

"Certainly, President of the Council,"

Hakana continued her report.

"I started the search within my habitat. I hoped to find out more by asking the eldest. I headed towards the Hakan Desert where I turned to the oasis "Wadi Aijana". I addressed Dichali, The One Who Speaks A Lot. But as she couldn't help me, she sent me to Kaga, The Chronicler. He lives in a cave located in the mountains of The Invisible Summits. Although he is the guard of all the gemstones of the deceased dragons, he couldn't help me either."

A surprised whisper rose among them.

"President of the Council, would you do me a favor? May I return to Kaga as soon as my work is done here? I'd love to be taught how to read the stones."

"Hakana, Daughter of the Desert, it is too early to come to a decision right now. But we don't want to leave you in the dark. The one, who is able to turn the sun has been found. Sandy, Draco and Stella's daughter, is the one who is able to turn the sun. Figuratively this means she is the dragon who is able to turn destiny."

This was a stunning revelation for Hakana.

"And now as we are complete, every single dragon who was mentioned by the Oracle in its prophecy is present, I suggest continuing with our tasks and complete our plan of action. Draco please inform

Hakana about her duties. Meeting adjourned."

STELLA

Silent Wings and Stella couldn't believe it. The legendary Ikechi, The Power Adama's, was Draco's father. What a remarkable revelation!

"Mum, do you know his story a bit more in detail?"

she asked eagerly.

"Well, only what is said at The Great Gatherings and in the dens."

"Which is?!"

"Many rotations before the Council of the Seven Stones was founded, Ikechi was the dragon who uphold law and order all over Muraco. He is Adama's brother even though he is many rotations younger. He was also out of Berhane and Erwaen's clutch but at a much later time. The Oracle appointed him to settled disputes. Broadly speaking, he was supposed to maintain law and order. It is said that he is a mighty creature."

"Is he still alive?"

Silly stared at her grandmother in disbelief.

"Of course! When such a legendary dragon is about to die this is a major event. Only selected family members and a guard of honor accompany the dragon to the site where he is going to rest for eternity. They sing funeral songs while letting the dragon enter the realm of the dead."

"Is it true that all dragons come to the same site in order to die? And is this really a secret cave which is located in the highest mountains in this world?"

Silent Wings asked curiously.

"Yes, that is as true as the fact that in this very cave you also find all the protective stones of every deceased dragon. It is called the Cave of the Sparkling Stones."

"This ceremony must be a fascinating spectacle."

Stella remarked greatly intrigued.

"Oh yes, definitely."

"As soon as the dragon has eventually died, his stone is taken out. As a matter of precaution, only The Guard of the Gemstones is able to do this. This gem will be embedded in the cave's wall. Thus, his entire knowledge is kept for future generations. The corpse will be taken by four members of the Guard to the Ten Thousand Islands of the Rising Sun where it will be handed over to the restless fire, Ahote-Hakan. Afterwards an extraordinary meeting takes place which is organized by the family. Every dragon is invited to join it. It is a festival of joy. We want to celebrate the soul's smooth transfer to its ancestors."

"Have you ever attended such a celebration?"

Stella asked her mother.

"No, I haven't."

"Talking of Ikechi. Do you know where he is right now?"

"It is said that his homeland lies far in the north, in The Cold Land. That isn't surprising."

"Why isn't it surprising?"

"Well, he is a gigantic ice dragon with dazzling white fur, massive paws and dark-blue talons. As a gemstone he has a huge nugget of gold which shines like the sun. His wings have the same color as his talons but they are translucent."

"Then he looks like Sparkle, doesn't he," Silly mused.

"That shouldn't surprise us. He is his grand-father, isn't he?" confirmed her mother.

"And my grand-father, too."

"Yes, and yours, too."

"But why did Ikechi give up his role as a law enforcer?"

"Well, during the course of the rotations the number of dragons in the world had increased. When making his decisions a few of the dragons felt neglected. Especially the dragons of the oceans kept complaining to the Oracle. They didn't really have any reasons. But this led to the new system. Nowadays each region of this world chooses their own representative. These present their habitats' interests in the newly established Council of the Seven Stones."

"And Ikechi, how did he feel about it? Did he feel betrayed?"

"How he felt, we don't know. The Council sometimes appointed him to support them as Adama's Power. But what we know is that shortly after, Gazalay had another litter of 3 little dragons. The father was Ikechi. One of these hatchlings was Draco."

"Amazing. And who were the others?" asked Silly curiously.

"One of the young didn't hatch. The second one was a beautiful green dragon girl. Her name was Abha. She disappeared shortly after she had found her gem. She was on her way to visit her mother.

"Oh, Adama!"

"Ikechi vanished soon afterwards. Neither of them have been seen since."

Silent Wings stared at her grandmother, lost in thought.

"Do you think there is a connection between Ikechi and his daughter's disappearance?"

"I've no idea."

"That is such a sad story, isn't it?"

"Yes and no at the same time," pondered Raiffa.

"Thanks to Gazalay and Ikechi we have a marvelous dragon among us. His name is Draco."

She turned to Stella with a bright smile. Stella blushed like a young dragon-lady.

"And as far as I know Abha's stone isn't in the Cave of the Sparkling Stones."

Thoughtfully Stella glared at her mother,

"I've one more question, Mum. Does Draco know that The Red is his half-brother?"

"I guess so. At The Great Gathering it was well known and Gazalay has never tried to keep it a secret. In contrast to Charc's father, she has never mentioned his name."

Stelle looked at her mother attentively.

"Mum, who is our father?"

RAIFFA

Raiffa was taken by surprise as Stella had put her question so bluntly to her. Her head was spinning.

"What am I supposed to say? I've been able to avoid this question for so many years, I was able to give evasive answers. Now that my daughters are grown up, I haven't expected that question anymore and now I'm getting caught after all these years."

Her body color changed from light-green to beige. And where her body used to be beige it turned snow-white. This happened a couple of times. The coral on her forehead became rose-colored. When she was finally able to calm down again the color of her body and of her jewel also turned to their usual color.

"Well, it is not really that important to know who your father is…"

Stella noticed that her mother was using the present tense.

"You had a wonderful childhood and you have become remarkable dragon-ladies. Silly, could I talk to your mother alone for a moment so that I can explain everything?"

"No grandmother, I'd like to hear that too. It also concerns me. I also like to know whose genes I have got."

Raiffa sighed deeply but then gave in.

"The Oracle's prophecy led me to the Ten Thousand Islands of the Rising Sun. It wasn't difficult to find my gemstone, my coral. It is a beautiful place there, my dear. You must see it one day. The palm trees, the dazzling white beaches, food in abundance …"

"Mum, don't get carried away!"

"Well, I decided to stay in this paradise a bit longer. I enjoyed the beach and the scorching sun on my scales. When it got too hot, I plunged into the turquoise-colored water. But I had the strange feeling as if someone or something constantly watched me. One sunset when the silver disk of the cold light got reflected off the pitch-dark surface of the waves, these suddenly got divided. A most impressive water-dragon joined me. His gem was made of silver. It looked like a nautilus. From the beginning on we got along very well. The only disadvantage was that he is nocturnal while I'm not. Initially we were able to overcome that difficulty. He could be on dry land during the night and I loved swimming."

"That's incredible! I cannot believe it. Since I know you, I've never seen you inside the water."

"That is correct. But before you were born, I was almost a water-dragon."

Silent Wings and Stella gazed at each other completely puzzled.

"And so, the inevitable happened. One day I noticed that I was pregnant. We kept thinking how we could see each other from time to time without leaving our own proper habitat. We found an atoll which seemed perfect for our purpose. I spent my time on dry land and Argento, that is his name, visited me as often as possible. But according to my taste that still wasn't often enough. Especially as it got dead-boring on this atoll. I decided to find a more interesting place for me and my hatchlings. I departed straight after one of his visits. It would take him some time to return. I looked for a home on Raiffa's Finger."

"And what was so bad about it? It is rather common that the female dragons raise their hatchlings on their own,"

Stella commented.

Her mother explained,

"But there is a dragon-law concerning hatchlings whose parents are from different habitats. It requires that these hatchlings have to be divided up between the parents. What I did was unlawful."

"But Mum, Bernadette and I we are shining example of desert dragons. What were we supposed to do in the ocean?"

Raiffa reluctantly answered,

"Well, you are not the only hatchlings of that clutch. You have two brothers."

Now Stella and Silent Wings very completely startled.

"It was obvious right after you had hatched. The two male dragons had webbed toes, their skin was totally different than yours. They were real sea dwellers. But I refused to believe that. I set up a schedule down to the last detail. During the day I wanted to look after you, the land dwellers, and during the night I wanted to look after my nocturnal sea dwellers. But that didn't work. I was exhausted in no of time. And in the meantime, Argento had figured out where I was living. He wanted to get his sons. It happened when we were hunting shortly before sunrise. A huge shadow leaped seemingly out of nowhere. Argento! He had already watched me for quite some time. He demanded his rights.

For me it was clear I wouldn't let my hatchlings go voluntarily."

"But grandmother, these were also Argento's kids and besides they were sea dwellers."

"Yes, my dear. You are right, I know. But at that time, I saw it differently. I decided to fight for my kids. As you can imagine, I lost out to him. He drowned me until I fainted. When I regained consciousness, I was lying on the beach. Argento and the two boys were gone. On that day I concluded that I would never touch water again."

"Have you ever seen your sons, our brothers, again?"

"No, never."

"I can't believe it! And you have never tried to find out where they are? Hinto or any other sea dweller could have helped you."

"Of course, I have tried that. It was easy for me at the time when I was still able to fly. At each and every Gathering I asked about them. And I was reassured that they are fine."

"Don't you ever long to see them, just once?"

"They are water-dragons. I vowed to myself never to swim again. I won't change my mind about it, I mean it."

Stella and Silent Wings said good-bye to Raiffa and then hurtled to the Council of the Seven Stones.
"I am not surprised anymore that you and your sibling are so different from each other,"
Stella told her daughter.
"But I wonder if Bernadette and I aren't strangely atypical of our family. Because if you have a look at our family tree there isn't a single desert dragon."
Silly had to smile.
"I am convinced if we go further back in the past, we will also find a desert dweller."
"May Adama answer our prayers."
They had a very entertaining journey as they were trying to find out who of Silly's sibling resembled which ancestor. This conversation made Stella forget her worries about Bernadette for a little while. After a few sunrises they arrived at the Assembly Place. Draco came hurrying towards them.
"Stella what are you doing here?"

Stella informed him about Bernadette's fateful position and her concerns about her sister. The others joined them gradually. They were full of righteous indignation about Charc's behavior. Furthermore, they were outraged because of their own incapability to defeat him.

"I could try to find something out about her,"

Rocket turned to Draco and Hinto.

"Since I know where they are hiding, I could observe them in their ambush. I'll be able to stay out of their sight. If Aunt Bernie is still captured, I will see that."

"But it is also important that we work on our strategy."

"I won't be long. It will be a short flight to get some information. I am going to use my rocket engine."

"So be it," Hinto agreed.

"Mum, I have to say farewell,"

Silent Wings informed her mother.

"Why farewell? I thought you wanted to help us rescuing Bernadette."

"That isn't my task. My task was to accompany you safely to this place. Without me you would have tried to help Bernadette on your own and you would have put yourself into great danger."

Stella watched her daughter thoughtfully. "You are right."

Stella said goodbye to her daughter with a tender nudge on her snout which made Silly feel rather embarrassed. Silent Wings leapt up, hind legs digging into the ground, and then spiraled up into the air and turned towards the Dragon-Head-Cliff.

BERNADETTE

Bernadette's belly had begun to swell. During the short moments when she wasn't tied, she touched her flanks and felt four eggs; two on each side. Due to the swelling of her belly it was necessary for her to go bathing more often in order to cast her skin. Charc waited impatiently for her skin as he wanted to produce more dragon-skin powder. Whenever The Red was absent his gang members were in ugly fights over who should get the skin. Bernadette seemingly has resigned to her fate but she sincerely hoped that Stella would find a way to help her.

"Oh Adama, please, I am also one of your ancestors' being. Protect me and my hatchlings. And please rescue us from the clutches of this unscrupulous monster as soon as possible."

As it was also in Charc's interest that neither Bernadette nor the eggs lacked anything she spent rather comfortable days under the given circumstances. She got meat, leaves and herbs to eat. The ideal food which is necessary for the growth of embryos. She could go swimming whenever she felt like it. She had a rather pleasant time apart from the fact that she was trapped by the most ferocious bastard known in this world who had mated with her again. It wouldn't take much longer anymore and the gestation period would be halfway through. There were even some short moments when she was looking forward to having her hatchlings until the moment that she remembered again who their father was. She pondered,

"We should leave soon. The further the pregnancy progresses the more immobile I will become. I won't be able to fly so far if he really wants to return to my first den. There he will notice that this sanctuary doesn't exist anymore. That could be an advantage for me. I will have to look for another home in an area where I know every corner. Maybe that will be my chance to escape."

Grimly The Red returned from his trip. Obviously, he had been unsuccessful. In his fury he killed another one of his companions.

"If he goes on like that, very soon there won't be anyone left from his Pink Brigade.'

After he had calmed down again, he turned to Bernadette,

"Well baby, your sight fills me with joy. Four wonderful stones are waiting for me. I guess, it would be very appropriate to regard you as the primordial mother of my stones. Three I already possess. Success is guaranteed and I won't have to go hunting anymore."

This statement made Bernadette lose her self-control. But Charc immediately gave a sign and five of his dragons dashed instantaneously towards Bernadette, grabbed her, tied her and even bound her jaws together again.

"And before I forget, we are shortly to return to our sweet home. It is just a precaution. I don't want you to become weak during the journey and we don't want to put our kids in danger, do we? Heh-heh!"

His filthy laughter made her stomach turn.

"And before I forget; of course, we are going to fly after sunset. Just in case that your family is looking for you, which I doubt. They probably think you are dead by now."

Bernadette stayed silent as each further word would have only been a waste.

ROCKET

Rocket had arrived at Lake Emerald. He had approached the lake from the south. Clouds of spray splashed up from the majestic waterfall and covered the region where it plunged down into the lake. Rocket skimmed over the water's fine spray. The outlet of the lake had cut a deep narrow gorge into the rocks over millions of rotations. The end of this torrent cascaded into a broad fjord which opened further on into the ocean. This was the place where Rocket had seen the Pink Brigade the last time.

Rocket made sure that he stayed unnoticed. He concealed himself behind a cloud where he leveled off, switched into a mode of hovering and at the same time he activated his gemstone, his cylinder, which was in charge of the ultraviolet radiation. Suddenly the different colors were distorted. The colder an object or a plant was, the more prominent were the blue and green colors to him whereas the warm living beings were perceived by him in rich orange and red. It didn't take long when he spotted a dragon, shining in bright orange. Of course, he couldn't see any details from this distance but he could tell that this dragon had taken off into the direction of the Oracle.

"Oh Adama, that can only be Charc searching another victim. What an audacity! This bastard is continually becoming bolder."

His growing outrage had almost pushed him off balance. A little later, he noticed further movements down below him. He could see the outlines of four dragons accompanying a fifth one who entered the water. All of them appeared to him in orange-red. The fifth dragon bathed for a long time. When there suddenly was an uproar the dragon had left the water and shook itself. It was immediately surrounded by the other dragons. Its color had changed to a light yellow since its skin had been cooled off by the water. The dragon was led back into the cave by the others. Rocket stayed a few more sunrises on his watching post before he decided to return. On his last day he observed the same scenario again. It was a riddle to him, he couldn't solve. Apart from that, nothing else happened and so he departed and dashed back to the Council.

A council meeting was convened immediately when Rocket arrived at the Assembly Place. He informed the Council members what he had seen. Stella couldn't contain herself,

"That was Bernie. He still keeps her captured. And she is pregnant."

The Council members including Draco were shocked by Stella's behavior. Apart from the Council members nobody was allowed to speak during the meetings. Hinto, who had recomposed himself before anyone else turned to Stella,

"Stella, Raiffa's Daughter, even though, you have just broken an unwritten rule I ask you to speak. These are unusual times which require unusual measures. Please go on."

Stella made an effort to regain her self-control again.

"Mr. President, Representatives of the Council of the Seven Stones, I am convinced that this dragon is my sister Bernadette. And I am also convinced that she is pregnant. Every female dragon who has been pregnant knows very well, how much the belly grows during pregnancy.

This makes the process of molting so necessary during that time. If a pregnant female has the opportunity to bathe, she will do that in order to keep her skin soft and smooth. This way the outer covering can be cast off more easily. If there is no water nearby, they roll in sand or mud."

"Are you saying that your sister has been raped?"

inquired Hinto, stunned.

"Well, Mr. President of the Council due to her personal history I just cannot imagine that my sister would have devoted herself voluntarily to one of these bastards."

"What kind of history?"

Stella told Bernadette's dreadful story.

Draco interrogated Stella,

"Do you mean he abused her so that he can easily get hold of the young generation and their gems?"

"That could be the case, couldn't it? This has already worked out well for him once before."

Hakana couldn't refrain from commenting, "This time it is even more convenient for him. He has mated with Bernadette, then he will wait until his offspring is mature enough to get their prophecies from the

Oracle and as a caring father, he will escort one kid after the other to Adama."
Draco muttered,
"I believe that he is capable of doing that."
"You say that in a way as if you knew him personally. Do you ?"
Yas asked curiously.
"No, I don't know him personally. But he is my half-brother, just to let those of you know who haven't known that yet. He is much younger than I am and we have never met each other. No, I've to correct that. That is not true. I met him once when we freed Sparkle from his claws. But in this case, I didn't care about our relationship. He had tortured my son and wounded him seriously. Whenever I saw my mother at The Great Gathering, she told us another cruel deed he had committed. He has no sense for right and wrong and obviously never a guilty conscience. But I also have to blame my mother a bit, she had never scolded him when he had tortured others. Once, he had bitten off a playmate's tail, she only said, "He has not yet left his childhood behind. He will stop doing these things when he's grown up." But as we can see now, he hasn't stopped doing these things.

Just the opposite. Things have become worse."

"Do you think your mother would let us know one of his blind spots? That might help us tracing him down,"

Stella thought aloud.

"I can't tell. He has acquired his strength with the help of his protective stone, as we all have. In addition, he possesses the bloodstones with their different qualities. He also takes advantage of these very thoroughly. And he doesn't feel obliged to stick to our codex. A dragon's life means nothing to him. But we, on the other hand, have to get him without killing him."

A murmur of approval went through the council.

"What do you think Stella, how far has your sister's pregnancy already proceeded?"

"Of course, I don't really know that. But if he mated with my sister successfully immediately after she got captured then she would be more than half way through the gestation period by now. In addition, I'd like to point out, that she won't be able to breed where she is staying right now. Bernadette needs a sandy cave or at least sandy ground and the appropriate temperature."

"Just to make sure that I've understood you correctly, Stella. This means that we have half a rotation left to rescue your sister before she is going to lay her eggs. Plus the time, the hatchlings need to grow up before they can fly to the Oracle in order to get their prophecies."

"Yes, I think that is quite right," confirmed Stella.

"I am terribly sorry for your sister but she will have to endure this situation a bit longer. We must set priorities. It is most important to develop a successful strategy first."

Hinto sounded genuinely regretful when he looked at Stella.

"Your Honor, and if we trapped him?" Hakana suggested.

"What's on your mind, Hakana?"

"Well, as I already mentioned, I had been in the Cave of the Sparkling Stones. We have to find a way to make him believe that he could find thousands of gemstones there. That might boost his greed. And then we could ambush him there."

"I thought we would try to defeat him on the ground. Wouldn't an aerial combat be an extremely risky thing to attempt?"

Hinto mulled over her suggestion, considering it from every angle.

"If we coordinate our strategy well, this could definitely be an advantage. We have to attempt the impossible."

Rocket had already run through different possible variations.

"And I could be the decoy."

Everybody turned to Sandy in great astonishment.

"Well, he knows me. Even though, I've found my stone he'll never think highly off me or think that I might be a powerful dragon with special skills. I will try to find him. Then I will make him believe that I've been outcasted by the dragon-world because I had betrayed my own brother. I am sure this might give me the chance to stay by his side for at least some time. Then I can mention the Cave of the Sparkling Stones in order to fuel his greed for the stones. That should be dead easy."

Hakana added,

"In any case, it is absolutely vital to inform Kaga about it."

"I can do that. And then it is about time we completed our strategy,"

Rocket urged the council.

"As soon as I am back, we can practice our aerial combat and then Sandy can set off."

GAZALAY

Gradually Gazalay also became concerned about her son's evil deeds.

"I'm afraid I might not have taken it seriously enough. But he is, after all, my son." She had just recently visited her friend, Raiffa, who didn't live far away from her on Raiffa's Finger. The time periods between the official Gatherings they considered as far too long. There is got to be time for a bit of gossiping. And so, it happened that Gazalay flew eastwards across the bay at regular intervals. Raiffa had always prepared some delicacies for her which Gazalay normally didn't have at her disposal.

As Raiffa was an exceptional expert for mixing dragon-skin powder for any type of physical weakness, dragons from all over the world came to see her. Being such an expert at blending and creating unique remedies, brought her the additional advantage to be very well informed about the happenings in the world. She received not only all kinds of information, unknown new healing herbs and powders but also these delicacies from various different areas as thank-you presents from dragons who had needed help.

This time she informed Gazalay about a frightening story which she had been told. Two dragon-ladies had been ambushed, which was terrible, but to keep one of them captured was highly reprehensible.

Raiffa also desperately wanted to know who The Red's father was. But Gazaly stayed silent as always.

"This time the visit was really unpleasant," Gazalay thought when she reached a picturesque cove close to her hiding place. Her chrysolite blazed in olive-green; evidence that she was thinking very hard.

"I am going to stay right here for some time. Everybody knows that I am Charc's mother. But I am not responsible for his deeds. I am also Draco's mother. He is my pride and joy and a fantastic son. I probably shouldn't have mentioned this so often to Charc. I told him that no one would ever be able to compete with his brother. That was obviously a big mistake. Charc has asked me over and over again who his father is. But I have never answered that question. Isn't he entitled to know the truth? I think, I've made countless mistakes. But he has been a grown-up dragon for a long time.

And at some point, you can't blame the mother any longer for the actions of a grown-up dragon."

Gazalay stayed on the beach until darkness fell. She was just about to leave when a huge dragon perched next to her.

"What are you doing here?"

A fiery red dragon with red eyes and black pupils folded its translucent black wings. It was this black color against which his red eyes seemed to form a dangerous signal.

"I wanted to visit you, baby."

His gemstones glinted in the moonlight. It was a spiral made of several gemstones which were all equal in size and perfectly round. They glowed in all colors of the rainbow; Yellow, orange, red then purple dark-blue, light-blue and finally turquoise and light-green. They stood in stark contrast to his red scales.

"I had not expected you to reappear once again."

"Well, Ickechi made it quite clear that I am no longer welcomed here on Muraco, The World of The White Moon. If he hadn't had the power, he had once received from Adama, he would never have been able to defeat me. But as you see you can always contrive ways and means."

Benishoson, Benisho's Descendant and Charc's father showed a cold, maniacal grin.

THE FAVORED FEW

While the others were discussing various tactics, childhood memories returned to Nero to torment him. He felt isolated and left out.

"I will try to contact Sparkle. Maybe that will cheer me up a bit."

Nero asked the High Council for permission. He obtained the approval, to be absent for a few sunrises. Relieved, he flew eastwards towards the coast.

Finding an ambush site and to determine a specific time, on which the entire operation would depend on, put him under immense pressure.

As soon as he had reached the shore, he tried desperately to contact his brother. The water temperature had dropped significantly. Small ice chunks were floating on the surface. While swimming in the icy water for several sunrises he tried to contact his brother again and again. During this time, he started to feel sluggish and became even a little lethargic. As the water temperature was still slightly above the frigid air temperature he preferred to stay inside the water. He made a final attempt to get in contact with Sparkle, but to no avail. Nero had forgotten that in The Cold Land the time of The Long Night had started and linked to that also the time for the winter sleep. The time of the year when all dragons in this region had already stored plenty of body fat and had curled up in sheltered dens in order to avoid the icy blizzards while waiting for the sun to return. Disappointed he departed the snowy landscape.

He addressed Yas, the representative of The Cold Land, and talked to him about his fatigue which had overcome him while trying to contact Sparkle.

"I wasn't aware of the fact that you wanted to communicate with your brother in The Cold Land. Of course, that wasn't possible. Before the blustery winds set in and the temperatures drop constantly below zero all the dragons put on a thick layer of fat in order to survive the extreme climate during The Long Night. The dragons are enjoying a good snooze right now."

"Now I know why Sparkle was always hungry."

Yas smiled,

"Yes, that is just the way we are; the dragons from the north,"
he acknowledged with a twinkle in his eyes. Nero became thoughtful,
"Does this also refer to The Invisible Summits?"
"But of course. Ask Hakana. She will definitely confirm how chilly it is up there. Above a certain altitude you'll find only eternal ice and snow."
"But how come that Kaga, The Chronicler, doesn't sleep?"
"That is his secret."
Nero walked over to Hakana.
"When you were over at Kaga's, were you suffering from the
cold?"
"Oh yes, definitely. Especially when I had to fly through the bitter cold clouds. It had been almost unbearable until I finally broke through the clouds and the sun touched my body again. It was still freezing but it was tolerable thanks to the sun.
"Thank you very much,"
he mulled over her comments and waddled away.
In the meantime, Draco was elected head of their project by The Favored Few. Together they worked out a battle tactic.

They assumed that Sandy would accompany The Red shortly before the attack. Therefore, they decided to be very careful not to put her life at risk."

"As soon as we can get into action Sandy is going to give Hakana a signal and then I will face Charc. We have to make hundred percent sure that we will neither jeopardize Kaga nor Sandy. Since we don't know if he can release his beam of light only individually or in combination with a jet of fire, we have to expect that he can do both at the same time. I am going to throw a beam of light directly onto his protective stone in order to distract him. And at the same time, I am going to send a beam of fire at his body. I am sure The Red will only shake himself and then he will burst into laughter about my lousy attempt to attack him. That will be the moment when I am going to disappear into the clouds while Rocket is going to show up instead of me. You, Hakana, you are going to appear right behind The Red. Diana is going to be on your right side whereas I am going to be on your left. Sandy you dive straight down into the clouds but stay in contact with Hakana and send her your rays to support her. We are going to aim at Rocket all at the same time. Rocket you have to amplify all these rays and release them towards The Red. And now we are going to practice this, down to the smallest detail, up to perfection. But please keep in mind there can always be some unpredictable incidents which might force us to change our tactic. Sandy and Hakana you will be our messengers. Well, let's get going."

They darted off to the mountain range where the Dragon Head was located. This was where they trained finding the appropriate dosage for their beams so that they could reach the accurate distance. On Nekan's desert ground they practiced their positions which they would occupy during the deployment. And then the most challenging part began; the aerial combat. It took them quite some time but finally, they had figured out their perfect positioning and even Draco was pleased.

Nero had retreated from the others. He had found the clearing where his family had broken their journey on their first trip to The Great Gathering. Perching on a cliff he slightly dozed off; almost like a meditation. When he woke up again, he felt wide awake. And most important, he had found a solution to his problem.

One sunset after their practice, Stella turned to Draco,

"I am convinced that Bernadette's gestation period is half over by now. She won't be able to lay her eggs where she is staying right now. They have to find her another retreat; a place Bernadette agrees on. We'd rather observe in which direction they are heading; or even better where exactly they are flying to. We have to make sure that we'll notice their departure otherwise it will be too late for us.

"We will send Rocket to Lake Emerald. He shall have a look at their hiding place," Draco decided.

SILENT WINGS

A light hum cut through the air. Gazalay and Benishoson turned around.

"Son," this is how Gazalay called Benishoson,

"may I introduce you to my grand-daughter Silent Wings?"

He mumbled his agreement,

"Sure."

"You can leave it up to me, Grandma."

Gazalay didn't like to be called grandma at all.

"I'll do that myself. Adama be with you! I am Silent Wings, Draco and Stella's daughter."

"Adama be with you! I am Benishoson, Descendant of Benisho."

He was very interested but didn't show it.

Silly felt confused. She had come to this place because she had received urgent pleas for help. Seeing her grandmother with a descendant of Benisho's that seemed to be a challenging issue. Was Silly supposed to rescue her grandmother from him? But above all she was absolutely intrigued to find out more about the past.

"Please forgive me for being so curious, Benishoson. But our Aunt Bernadette used to tell us legends and myths."

Gazalay flinched as Silly mentioned Bernadette's name.

Silly continued,

"One of your ancestors is Benisho, The Shining. Is it all true what the myths tell us? Nobody has ever known what gemstone he had possessed. Neither has anyone known how he had received the skill to capture the sunlight and to amplify it a thousand times in just one ray before emitting it. I've asked myself over and over again how that was possible and if that really is the truth. You, as one of his descendants, should know the answer, shouldn't you?"

"Well, I don't know the whole truth. But I am also able to capture sunlight and to emit amplified light. That skills runs in the family."

Gazalay flinched again.

"And what about his protective stone?" Silly kept asking eagerly.

"It was a white diamond with black inclusions."

This time not only Gazalay flinched but so did Silent Wings. Silly quickly composed herself.

"And could you explain how you do that with the rays?"

"You are really curious, aren't you, young dragon-lady? I think for today I've told enough. Maybe next sunrise, don't you agree, Gazalay,"

and once again Gazalay flinched.

BERNADETTE

The Red, his Pink Brigade and Bernadette had set off for Bernie's old homeland. They crossed the south continent heading northwest. They moved continuously along the edge of The Green Canopy. Their destination was the protective jungle where they wanted to take a rest shortly before sunrise. They traversed the strait in the south of the isle. The very island where Rocket had found his gem. But suddenly Charc reversed directions. He turned northward.

"You didn't think that I would pass the Assembly Place, did you baby? You should know me by now. I am not that stupid."

Bernadette silently had to agree with him. Indeed, she had hoped he would have done exactly that.

"Well, I can reassure you. We are flying to Dragon Head Cliff first, then I will verify whether the coast is clear before we will seek our old sweet home."

Bernadette's hope, to get rescued, were immediately dashed again. They approached the shelter place in the mountain where the Red had already been hiding during the time of The Great Gathering. As soon as they were inside the hideout, they tied Bernadette. The risk that she was discovered by one of the members of the Council of the Seven Stones was too high. She had to stay out of sight. So, he set off on his own. Coming from the north he veered west along the west coast of the northern continent toward Bernadette's former cave right after sunset. He circled above the mountain and couldn't make out any danger for neither himself nor his companions. From this distance he couldn't see that Bernadette's den was destroyed. The Red considered the situation as riskless. Thus, he took the same way back on the following sunset.

"Well, baby, nothing will deter you any longer from laying your eggs. I just have to be a bit more patient before I'll have four further protective stones to adorn my head. What a very promising perspective for my future. He-he-he."

If Bernadette hadn't been tied up, she would have attacked him right then and there.

ROCKET

As soon as he had arrived at Lake Emerald, Rocket started to inspect the entire area around the lake, the river and the opening to the sea. He observed the cliff which had been occupied by one of Charc's companions once before. With the help of all of his cylinders he tried to capture any kind of signal which might correspond to a dragon. But only minor creatures were bustling around. Their body temperature was sometimes higher sometimes lower.

"What shall I do now? I am too late. They can be anywhere. Aunt Bernie needs a sandy cave for her eggs. This is what Mom said. The Hakan Desert and the Nekan Desert would be ideal for that. But I don't have enough time to visit both of them. If they are hiding in a cleft, I won't be able to find them anyway."

Reluctantly, he abandoned his search. Darkness was already falling. But he loved to look from above onto the dragon world Muraco especially after sunset. He soared straight into the sky as he always did. He had decided to call off his search when he was between the Assembly Place and the

Dragon Head Cliff. When he reached his destination, he leveled out and leisurely glided over the treetops.

"What is that?"

A whole bunch of dragons flapped away westwards coming from the Dragon Head Cliff.

"Well, if that isn't.... I will observe them and find out where they are heading to. I am sure that this is Charc with his Brigade and Aunt Bernie. No other dragon would fly after sunset if it could be avoided. And a flock of dragons that isn't normal either, except in times of The Great Gathering. But that is the only time."

Rocket followed them towards the west, along the coast to the south until they reached the edge of Nekan Desert where they disappeared into a mountainside.

"If that isn't the breeding place."

Rocket also noticed a small river which flowed westward into the open sea. He stayed for another sunrise and observed the happenings. He was convinced that he had discovered The Red and Aunt Bernie in their new hideout. He dashed directly to the east. The Assembly Place wasn't far away.

SANDY

Sandy and Hakana had mapped out a detailed plan. Sandy should convince Charc that the Cave of the Sparkling Stones would be an immeasurable source for him, providing countless of protective stones. All he had to do was to get rid of The Chronicler.

Meanwhile, Hakana was supposed to wait for Sandy's rays while hiding behind the protective clouds. This way they would be able to communicate with each other. But as the time approached Sandy started to have second thoughts and wondered how she could persuade Charc that the Cave of the Sparkling Stones would be a true treasure for him. It seemed downright reckless. He must have been aware of the fact that the cave was guarded and protected. But first of all, she had to find him. Which meant that she had to make sure that he would find her. Rocket had explained his sister where he had seen the Pink Brigade. Sandy still needed a plausible explanation; Why was she exactly at this place just then?

Sandy and Hakana had given Bernadette's former den a wide berth before they headed towards the hideout. They were coming from the open sea, where they parted company well in time. Now Sandy was resuming her journey on her own.

"Hakana, can you hear me?"

"Yes, loud and clear."

"I just wanted to make sure, that everything is all set."

"Don't worry. I am here,"

Hakana acknowledged reassuringly,

"You can count on me."

Sandy approached the den with great caution when suddenly a red dragon appeared next to her. Fear grabbed her immediately.

"Hello baby. I haven't seen you for a while. What a pleasant surprise. Why are you looking so scared? Do you have a guilty conscience? He-he-he!"

"Charc, what are you doing here?"

"I could ask you the same question. So, what are you doing here? As I can see, you have found your stone. What a pity, your stone would have suited me also very well," he sneered.

"But be serious now. What exactly are you doing here?"

"Because of you my family has outcasted me, as I had betrayed my own brother. But the Oracle gave me my prophecy anyway. And since the day I found my gem, I've been exploring the world."

Charc's thoughts started spinning. Would she be an advantage for him if he took her with him? How could she be useful to him? Ideally, she would also provide him with some eggs. In the worst case he could make dragon-skin powder out of her.

"Well, then come with me. You can stay with me and my companions."

His suggestion made Sandy feel on edge since she couldn't understand his reasons.

"Hakana, he took the bait. He is taking me with him."

"Great. Keep it up!"

After a short time, they reached the new shelter which Bernadette had chosen for her egg deposition. Whenever Charc was out and about the Pinks allowed her to see her kids' grave in the former den. She had just returned from one of those visits when The Red, accompanied by Sandy, entered the cave.

"Sandy, what are you doing here?"

Bernadette jumped up to her feet and gasped in great astonishment.

"Aunt Bernie, how did you get here?"

Sandy had to pretend to be surprised, as if she knew nothing. Even though she knew exactly why Bernadette was here. The Red butted in,

"Well, ladies, you will have enough time for your chitchat later on. Sandy, now it is your task to help your aunt. Pregnant dragons need all kinds of support; especially female support. He-he-he."

"You returned to him on your own free will?" Suspicion was born immediately.

"You work with this bastard? And I thought you have changed!" Bernadette was outraged.

Before Bernadette was able to continue Sandy interrupted her.

"You know very well that my family has outcasted me because I betrayed Sparkle. I don't have any other choice. I also want to belong to someone."

"The Red, he of all dragons! I didn't expect you to stoop to staying with him and the Pink Brigade," she snorted.

Desperately Sandy tried to give her aunt a hint by winking. It was necessary to stop Aunt Bernie talking. She was lucky.

Somehow Bernadette got the clue. She didn't continue speaking, even though she didn't understand Sandy's behavior. But Bernadette's thoughts started racing frantically.

"What is Sandy up to? I remember so well how caring she was looking after Sparkle. Was she just pretending to be the lovely sister? Was she still The Red's accomplice at that time? I will play according to her rules. But I will also watch her very carefully."

A few sunrises passed by. During a quiet evening, even The Red had stayed in the den, Sandy dared an approach.

"Aunt Bernie do you remember, when we were little, you were telling us all kinds of stories before we were going to sleep? My favorite one was about the Cave of the Sparkling Stones."

Bernadette knew very well that she had never spoken about this cave.

"Sandy must be completely out of her mind to mention the dragon's shrine right here, of all places!"

Charc immediately pricked up his ears.

"What about this cave?"

Bernadette tried to stop Sandy.

"Sandy, that's enough. You can't tell him the story about the Cave."

Now Charc got really interested.

"Well baby, your Uncle Charc is looking forward to hearing this story."

Sandy started to tell the story,

"In the mountain range The Invisible Summits there is the Cave of the Sparkling Stones. It is guarded by The Chronicler, Kaga…"

Bernadette didn't believe her ears. Sandy was indeed Charc's accomplice.

NERO

"Rocket, can you spare a minute?"

Nero took his brother aside. The other Favored Few saw Nero talking vividly to Rocket. First Rocket looked skeptical, then thoughtful before he finally nodded and then surged into the sky where he disappeared in the clouds.

"What was that all about?" Draco demanded to know.

"Daddy, trust me. Rocket does something for me. He is going to be back in a few sunrises."

"Oh Adama! I hope for you that this is of vital importance," Draco hissed and then hurried off.

"Oh Adama! It is of vital importance," Nero mumbled to himself.

During Rocket's absence Nero spent a lot of time with Yas, the representative of The Cold Land.

SANDY

"He is determined to fly to the Cave, to kill The Chronicler and to get as many gems as he can carry. The most valuable ones he wants to insert right then and there."

"I see. I will depart immediately to inform Kaga. And you try to slow Charc down whenever possible. You are a female dragon so you are able to put on an act. Take advantage of that."

"I will. Hakana, you have to fly to the Council. He keeps aunt Bernie in captivity and six members of the Pink Brigade watch her continuously. The other six members are constantly out and about. Maybe we have a chance to rescue her."

"Sandy, I guess the Council will make their decision according to the urgency of the matter. Adama be with you! And Sandy, as soon as you arrive, we'll get in contact. I will let you know the way and give you every assistance I can."

"All right," Sandy confirmed.

From then on Sandy was left on her own.

Once again Charc decided to leave just after sunset. He knew the mountain range The Invisible Summits, since his first hide-out had been on Chendris. The very continent where also the mountain range was located. They had steadily made their way along the coast. There was no point for them to raise themselves higher up into the frigid cold. If Charc had known about the precious treasures which were hiding in there, he would have removed the entire mountain range stone by stone. As usual, they avoided the Assembly Place by circling far around it. Then they took the shortest way which meant that they had to fly directly across Draco's cliff. Each time when they were about to take off again, at around sunset, Sandy tried to postpone their departure. Once she had pretended to have an injured wing. That almost went wrong as The Red had given her some dragon-skin powder in order to stimulate her performance. She just managed to let it slip unnoticed into the deep sea where it disappeared.

"I've to think of better excuses."

She hoped with all her heart that Hakana would arrive before them as Hakana could fly before as well as after sunrise.

SILENT WINGS

Benishoson, The Descendant of Benisho, Gazalay, The Mysterious, and Silent Wings were still in the little cove when the sun rose. Benishoson woke up first, he had a good stretch before he dived into the water to catch his prey which he devoured delightfully as soon as he was back on dry land. He gave a loud uninhibited burp when turning to Gazalay watching her slit-eyed,

"To be honest baby, I've not come to visit you. I am here to see my son. I am really curious how he has turned out."

Gazalay's colorful body, consisting of turquoise, green and light-blue, looked suddenly slightly faded.

"Do you know where he's staying right now or what he's doing?"

"I don't know where he's staying at the moment. The last information I got about him was that he had just kidnapped three dragon-kids. And before that he had already kidnapped some other dragon-kids. He killed them in the wake of stealing their gemstones. This is your son! You can be proud of!"

"Well, we live in a world where this is a common behavior. Everyone has to look after themselves."

Silent Wings had listened to their conversation in great astonishment. Both of them were so outraged that they had completely forgotten about her.

"But that doesn't mean that we kill kids or other dragons."

"And why not? Sometimes it can be of some use. And sometimes it just can be nice to see others in discomfort and helplessness."

"And that's why I have never told Charc who his father is."

Smoke trailed from Benishoson's nostrils. He turned his head towards the rising sun and suddenly shot a bright ray of light, from the center of his spiral, right in front of Gazalay's claws. The sand melted immediately. She jumped back, her heart pounding frantically.

"This is just a little warning. You will never do anything that I don't' like."

He raged,

"Did you understand that?"

"Of course, I did. There is no reason to scream."

And again, smoke trailed from Benishoson's nostrils.

"I will make sure that my son gets to know who his father is. And that he can be proud of his ancestors. And you baby, you know now how my rays function."

Silly nodded, struggling not to panic. Benishoson glared at both of them through his red eyes, spread his mighty wings and took off. As if to prove his power he boiled the water surface spiral-shaped with his ray. Gazalay and Silent Wings stayed behind deeply shocked. Silly could hardly bring out a word,

"Now we've two of them. I've to fly to the Council and inform them at once."

Gazalay recomposed herself,

"Sure, do that, Love."

A few sunrises later Silent Wings perched on the Assembly Place. She asked to schedule a meeting so that she could report her story immediately. The council members hadn't even settled down when she already started talking.

"Benishoson, Charc's father, has arrived on Muraco. He is looking for his son. He is as vicious as The Red."

"I thought Ikechi had defeated him and banished him from our world. His desire to see his son must be very strong. Or maybe he has another reason for coming. I can't see Benishoson as a caring and loving father."

HInto looked around,

"Ikechi retreated many rotations ago. We don't know where he is staying. We will wait for Rocket to return. He can start looking for both of them."

Draco peered thoughtfully at his son Nero. "Do you already have an idea when and where we can ambush The Red?"

Yes, I do. But you will need a bit more patience."

SPARKLE

Sparkle had reached The Cold Land during a time which was called The Time Before The Long Night. His gnawing hunger surprised even himself. He went hunting from sunrise to sunset. Above the water, under water everywhere where he could trace some prey. Suddenly he startled. Underneath him he noticed a hole in the ice which was covered by blood. Obviously, blood had been dripping off a body which had dragged itself out of the hole and then lifted itself up into the air. But the blood hadn't stopped dripping onto the ice.

"I'll follow the trace,"
Sparkle decided.
"When I find this creature, I can finally eat as much as I want. According to the amount of blood it has lost, it must be a gigantic beast. It has to be somewhere around here. And then I only have to pick it up."

But that wasn't the case. The trace had disappeared when he reached a rocky mountain range. He flew back and forth over and over again. But the track was gone. After quite some time he finally was lucky again. He discovered a small red stain on the white snow. It was right in front of a cave.

"Shall I just enter? A hurt animal which feels cornered could become rather dangerous; even for a dragon. Regarding the blood drops it can't be a small animal." Sparkle weighed the odds.

"Hello, anyone in here?"

Only a faint groan was uttered as an answer. With great caution Sparkle advanced further into the den. There he was lying. A gigantic dragon with white fur dark-blue talons and translucent dark-blue wings. Most conspicuous was his gemstone. A huge gold nugget sat enthroned on his forehead. Almost as conspicuous was the wound at his belly. Blood was still oozing out of it. The wound had the shape of a circular hole.

"I can help you!"

The mighty dragon groaned through gritted teeth,

"Then you have to hurry up. I haven't much time."

Since his own recovery Sparkle always has had the most important remedies with him. He rummaged through them frantically until he found a shortened piece of bamboo cane in which he carried Rubi's Water. This is how he called the liquid her gemstone could produce. He poured some of it right into the open wound. The dragon winced and gasped for breath. Then Sparkle got a paste that had been made out of Rubi's ground dragon-skin. He rubbed it around the sensitive wound. And finally, he took some of Stella's ground powder and placed it together with some snow into a small pot, made of bamboo. With a well-dosed jet of fire, he melted the snow and made his patient drink the hot liquid.

"Oh Adama! I'm sure this will help."
Sparkle swore to himself,
"I am going to nurse this impressive dragon back to health. I am going to stay here by his side just the way Sandy did it for me."

HAKANA

Hakana had already left the Assembly Place when Silent Wings arrived. Therefore, Hakana didn't know that Benishoson had returned to Muraco, carrying out his evil deeds. Her goal was to get to The Invisible Summits as fast as possible. She had to inform Kaga immediately about Charc's intention to come to the Cave of the Sparkling Stones. She stopped to rest on The Telfi's main island only for a brief moment before she continued flying across the estuary climbing further into the sky. The temperature dropped considerably. Blizzards hampered her journey. Her wings became stiff and she was barely able to breath. Hakana slowly realized, with a sense of growing desperation, that her last visit was during the time of the Warm Sun and not during the dead of winter. The boundless vastness of white peaks glowed in the golden sunrise. The outstanding beauty of the wild landscape intrigued her greatly. And it was Kaga who had been chosen by this gorgeous area to live right here. But now there was no hope of getting through up to the summits. Nobody would be able to survive these icy temperatures, the blizzards and the thin air unless one was especially equipped for these conditions. Hakana didn't know what to do. Should she return to the Council and rather support The Favored Few? But that would mean, that she had to leave Sandy on her own with The Red. She made her decision. She would hide in the lower and warmer area waiting there for Sandy and her guides.

BENISHOSON

After Benishoson had left Gazalay he followed the shore north. He crossed the ridge which separated the coast from the Nekan Desert. Nothing slipped his excellent eyesight. And so, he also noticed the group of pink dragons flying along the shore heading north. He followed them. It was a group of rundown dragons which provoked his disdain. He increased the beat of his wings and then swooped down next to the leading dragon.

"Oh Adama! You scared me, boss."

"I am not your boss."

Benishoson turned towards him,

"Well, have a closer look. Aren't there a few differences which differentiate me from Charc? If he is your boss."

"Oh yes, of course. You are larger than him and you have a completely different gemstone. To be precise, you have many different stones."

"See?! Well done! I am sure you can also tell me where I can find your boss, who is my beloved son, by the way."

"The Red is your son?"

he asked puzzled.

"He has always told us that he doesn't know who his father is."

"That's the truth. He doesn't know. And now I'll tell him. So, where is he?" he demanded sharply.

"He and Sandy are on their way to Chendris, to the mountains of The Invisible Summits. They want to find the Cave of the Sparkling Stones."

"What kind of cave is that?"

"I am not sure about it. But if he finds this cave, he will be Muraco's most powerful dragon."

Benishoson listened carefully. He didn't regret looking for his son. But this was the moment when his priorities changed.

"Oh Benisho! You rendered me a wonderful service."

The Descendant of Benisho veered east.

SPARKLE

While The Long Night was falling and the biting winds were whipping the land outside the cave, inside the cave, Sparkle's nursing concept started to have successful effects. The grievous wound slowly began to heal and the dragon gradually regained his vitality.

"Please let me know who you are. What's your name? I'm so grateful and if I also knew who I should be grateful to, I'd be very happy."

"I am Sparkle, Draco and Stella's son,"
proudly, he mentioned his parents' names. His patient smiled,

"I am Ikechi, Adama's Power, and Draco's father."

Sparkle stared at him in great surprise. He was completely stunned.

"Wow, then you are my grandfather!"
he burst out in great astonishment.

"Yes, that seems to be the case," smiled Ikechi softy.

"We are direct descendants of Berhane and Erwaen. That is something to be very proud of, Junior."

"But I thought all dragons that live on Muraco are direct descendants of them."

"Yes, at the beginning. But then some of them mate with the inhabitants of the ocean and therefore there are some crossbreeds too."

"Is that bad?"

"No, of course not. But a few of these hatchlings gathered only disadvantages. Their disadvantages outweigh the advantages."

"Neither Mum nor Dad have ever mentioned that. Aunt Bernadette told us all these stories. But I've the impression quite a few stories are still missing."

Ikechi muttered rather to himself,

"My own grandchild found me during my weakest moment. Thank you so much, Junior. I don't know where I would have been now without your help."

"That goes without saying. How did that happen? Such a wound at the underbelly is rather peculiar, isn't it?"

"That's probably true. But here in The Cold Land you find the finest delicacies only under water, which is unfortunately also the most dangerous area to go hunting. Especially as I still have some foes down there. They are just waiting for me to enter the chilly water."

"Honorable Ikechi, may I propose something?"

"Go ahead."

"Obviously your wound has healed and we have both sufficient fat reserves to make it until the next Melting Waters arrive. Therefore, I suggest flying to the Council of the Seven Stones. There I can look for my sister, Rubi. She is also called The Blood of the Earth. She will be able to nurse your injuries completely. If I don't find her, I can still ask my Grandmother Raiffa or my Mum, Stella, to give me some dragon-skin powder."

Ikechi pondered for a moment,

"That is a great idea, Sparkle. I am looking forward to seeing their faces when entering the Council of the Seven Stones."

Indeed, their arrival at the Assembly Place produced gasps of amazement. Draco peered at Sparkle and Ikechi in great astonishment. He could only shake his head. As Sparkle took after his mother concerning his appearance it was remarkable to see the resemblance between these two. There were only few minor distinguishing characteristics. Ikechi had a nugget of gold whereas Sparkle possessed a cream color opal with inclusions which were punctiform and shined in all colors of the rainbow. One had golden brown eyes and the other light blue ones. Ikechi's talons and wings were dark-blue while his grandson's were cream-colored. What they had in common was the big dark-blue snout.

Yas, the representative of The Cold Land welcomed him first.

"My friend, it has been a very long time since we've heard from you. It's so good to see you."

They hugged and nudged each other noses with a bright smile.

Hinto waddled towards them,

"Ikechi, Adama's Power, wonderful to see you."

His eyes lighted up for a brief moment but the glimmer immediately vanished again.

Ikechi nodded his head which was barely noticeable.

"President of the Council."

Gradually all of them appeared on the Assembly Place. Sparkle was really surprised to see his mother here as well as his sister, Silent Wings. Nero and his inseparable companion, Diane, strolled leisurely towards the place. But at the sight of Sparkle his eyes grew wide and he lost his composure immediately.

"Sparkle!" he exclaimed incredulously, "Where do you come from? I've tried to contact you several times. You look good. What are you doing here?"

"Nero, one after the other. All things will be explained. May I introduce you to Ikechi, Adama's Power. He is our grandfather."

"Oh boy, oh boy, Sparkle! You are always good for a surprise!"

"Well, actually we were on our way to grandmother Raiffa. But as Mum is already here, she might as well have a look at Ikechi's wound."

And again, a glimmer showed in Hinto's eyes for a very brief moment.

Stella reacted immediately,

"Come with me. I will be able to help you, Ikechi."

"Ikechi, Adama's Power, the Council wants to talk to you about a very important matter. We are meeting at the hour of sunset,"

Hinto informed them while obstructing their way.

"As you wish, President of the Council."

Ikechi nodded his head and then left accompanied by Stella and Sparkle.

SANDY AND CHARC

As Hakana had already failed previously, so did Sandy now; due to the frigid temperatures and the fierce winds which whipped them unmercifully. Ice crystals flew into her eyes and made them continuously water. A layer of ice had formed on her wings which made it impossible for her to move. Charc had no problems with these demanding challenges. But he was forced to acknowledge the fact that Sandy wasn't able to find the cave under these circumstances. This led him to the decision to wait down at the shore until it was possible again to penetrate the biting cold in the height; just as Hakana had decided earlier on. The area The Red chose for his hideout was very well-known to Sandy. It used to be Charc's former ambush where he had stayed with his gang.

Sandy kept trying to contact Hakana, but to no avail. One sunrise she heard a signal. "Sandy, where are you? Can you hear me?"

Sandy tried to suppress her joy and to keep a straight face.

"Hakana, where are you? I couldn't reach you. I was starting to get desperate."

"I had to postpone my search for Kaga and his cave. I just wasn't able to cope with these appalling weather conditions. I am on The Telfi's main island now. And I'm waiting for the time of The Gentle Wind to come to the mountains."

"We're also waiting."

"You are saying, we are waiting? Is The Red with you?"

"Certainly. He is on the beach in front of me."

"Oh Adama, help us! There was just a red dragon hovering above me. He looked so much like Charc! I thought it was him."

"What does that mean?"

"That means that we have two Reds on Muraco. I can only think of one more dragon who that could be. That's Benishoson, the Descendant of Benisho. the one, Ikechi had sent into exile on another world. And that means that he has found a way back into our world."

"Oh Adama, please help us!"

"Sandy we'll stay in contact. I have to think."

Hakana was in a quandary – should she inform the Council that Benishoson had returned, or shouldn't she? Of course, the Council had to know this but the time would be too short to fly to the Assembly Place and to be back before the Time of the Melting Water set in. The Favored Few would be coming soon anyway.

"I will stay right here," Hakana decided. It seemed to be the most reasonable solution for her.

BENISHOSON

After Benishoson had found out the rough direction his son had been off to, nothing stopped him any longer to get to The Invisible Summits. Together with his son he would find the cave one way or another. And then he would take advantage of these stones all by himself. To put it mildly, it might even include the death of his son.

He had just crossed The Telfi's main island as well as the estuary which separated the string of islands from Chendris. He knew that The Red had company and he was convinced that an average dragon wouldn't be able to get to the cave under these weather conditions. That meant they had to wait for the Time of the Melting Water. And this gave him enough time to find them. He would scan the island in straight lines to make sure he'd cover the area methodically without missing any patches. It didn't take him a long time. Benishoson was on his way to the southern tip of the peninsula when he suddenly spotted two dragons flying underneath him. He dived straight down at a tremendous speed, performed a spiral dive until he was right in front of Charc's snout where he leveled out and then leisurely hovered in the air. Head to head they flapped next to each other standing in mid-air. Sandy couldn't believe her eyes. Two identical, red dragons one a bit bigger than the other. Neither of them was in any way inferior to the other. The only difference was their protective stone. A star-shaped black diamond with bloodstones at its tips and a spiral made of gemstones which glowed in all colors of the rainbow. The Red snorted in alarm,

"Who are you? Who is blocking my route?"

"I am Benishoson, The Descendant of Benisho, and Charc's father. I've come to find my son."

For a short moment The Red was speechless,

"You are late, Benishoson. I am Charc, Gazalay's son. Should I also be your son, then it is my pleasure."

"Right you are. You are our son."

"And why haven't you come any earlier?"

"Different adverse circumstances kept me from coming. But with the help of some mates I was able to overcome these."

In great astonishment Sandy had been listening to their conversation and sensed something was amiss.

Benishoson sneered,

"Don't you want to introduce me to this charming dragon-lady?"

"This is Sandy, Draco's daughter. Draco is my half-brother."

And now it was Charc who sneered in exactly the same manner his father had just done.

"She works as a guide here on Chendris."

"And where is she guiding you to?"

Neither The Red nor Sandy answered his question. Benishoson noticed that he still had to put in a good deal of energy to win his son's confidence.

NERO

As soon as Rocket had reached the Assembly Place, he talked to Nero. He seemed to be delighted about Rocket's information. Then he went to see Draco.

"In thirty days, we will be able to set off for The Invisible Summits. Rocket is going to show us the way to the cave which is guarded by Kaga."

"Well, my son, so be it. Adama, give us the strength to defeat The Red."

Draco mentally ran through a range of scenarios. The starting position had changed. The situation was completely different now than originally assumed. Benishoson had returned and was now looking for his son. In the worst case that could mean that they had to deal with two opponents. Ikechi had also returned. But was he still as strong as he used to be? Especially now that he had been injured so badly. Had his wound already healed completely? Could he take the responsibility to let his father fight with them under these circumstances? This question was answered just a little later. After the meeting with Hinto, Ikechi informed The

Favored Few that he'd also join the strike force. He would primarily take care of Benishoson in case they encountered both opponents at the same time.

Thanks to Stella's skills, Ikechi had completely regained his vitality. Only a small circular scar was left on his belly that bore witness to the attack.

And then, the time had come. Nero gave the signal for their departure. Rocket was supposed to scan the area so that they wouldn't meet Charc too early. He informed Hakana about the exact location of the cave which he had received from Kaga earlier on. Hakana forwarded the information on to Sandy and begged her to delay their departure as long as possible.

But the Time of the Melting Water came soon. Sandy didn't see any possibility to postpone their departure any longer. She informed Charc that she was ready to set off. He turned to his father,

"Well Benishoson, I think it is about time to part again. It was very nice to get to know you. But being grown-up dragons, we should now go our own ways again."

"But son, we've just found each other after such a long time. I don't want to leave you yet,"
answered The Descendant of Benisho with a broad grin on his face.

The Red couldn't contradict without raising suspicion. Thus, all three of them raised themselves into the air.

"Hakana we are on our way." Sandy emitted her rays.

"Take your time, Sandy. The Favored Few have left as well but they aren't here yet."

Sandy guided father and son from the south end of Chendris towards the north until they reached a broad mountain ridge obstructing their way. Snowcapped mountains rose into the sky. They soared even higher up into the air until they broke through the clouds. A few peaks pierced through the white glory. Even though the sun was shining it was freezing cold. Sandy who was a desert dweller was almost at the limits of her endurance. Nevertheless, she followed the gray-white peaks towards the east. This part of The Invisible Summits separated North Chendris from South Chendris. When they reached the point where this mountain range merged with the mountain range stretching along the coast, she veered to the south.

"Don't you think you've just taken a detour?"

Charc hissed grimly at Sandy.

"Of course, this is a detour. I assume that Kaga expects intruders coming from the south rather than the north."

"What are you talking about?"

Benishoson pretended to be very curious.

One could literally see how The Red was racking his brain. But then his decision was made. He would trust his father and let him in on his secret.

"We are flying to the Cave of the Sparkling Stones. I am sure you have heard about it. Sandy knows the location. We are going to collect all the gemstones which are stored there."

"But the cave is watched, isn't it?"

"Yes, there is a guard, with the name of Kaga. If Kaga doesn't let us enter, we'll have to apply force to get in."

Benishoson was almost proud of his offspring. That was a guy to his taste. What a shame that he had other plans for his son and the little one. With all these stones Ikechi would no longer be a danger for him if he ever appeared again. But even without these protective gemstones, it would have been difficult for Adama's Power to defeat him, Benishoson, The Descendant of Benisho, as he had some allies here on Muraco.

"Hakana, we are almost there,"

Sandy reached out to Hakana with her mind, who reassured her instantaneously,

"That's all right. Keep on flying. Adama be with you!"

"Adama be with you. I hope this plan will work out."

"It's a good plan."

Sandy had turned to the south. In this area the mountains were even more imposing. A few shreds of clouds got caught at the summits and then rolled slowly down, on the south side of the mountain range, where they covered the foothills. In the far distance they spotted a dragon leisurely drifting over the mountain peaks.

"If that isn't the legendary Kaga. Come son, let's give him hell."

Panic gripped Sandy. Desperately she sent her rays to Hakana.

"They have spotted Kaga. They are going to kill him!"

She perceived Hakana's answer mentally.

"Keep calm, Sandy. Whatever happens, stay calm and follow my instructions. They won't kill him before they haven't entered the cave. And until they get there, they'll still have to overcome a few obstacles."

"Oh Adama, if only it works out well."

The two red dragons hurtled towards Kaga. His mountain-crystal glinted in the sunlight. Benishoson rose to speak,

"My name is Benishoson, The Descendant of Benisho, The Shining Light. This is my son Charc. We want you to lead us into the Cave of the Sparkling Stones."

"Hmm, so you want. But neither of you looks like as if you are about to die. And in that case, there is no reason for me to take you to the cave."

"If life is dear to you, I think there is definitely a reason for you to do so."

"I am Kaga, The Chronicler and The Keeper of the Gemstones. I've sworn by the name of Adama to guard and protect these."

"Well, then we don't have a choice. We'll find it without your help."

Charc's stones had begun to glow. In his rage he didn't notice that Kaga had given Sandy a quick nod.

"Hold it! We don't have to kill him now. I know the entrance to the cave. Maybe he has some important information for us."

The two red dragons thoughtfully considered her suggestion.

"She is right. Well, then show us the entrance. And you, chosen by Adama as The Chronicler, come with us."

Sandy took the lead and then landed on a platform in front of the cave's entrance. Benishoson pushed her out of his way.

"You stay here. We are going on our own."

The Descendant of Benisho strode first towards the cave, when he suddenly heard a suspicious noise inside the rock. It vanished as quickly as it had come. Benishoson advanced further towards the cave's mouth when a hard and painful blow struck him. Immediately he took a step backwards. He waited until he had recovered and then tried once more. But it happened again.

"What's going on?"

Charc nudged his father out of the way. But he experienced just the same. Painful strokes jolted through his body.

"Well, I guess it is about time that you let us enter your cave. Otherwise this little dragon is going to pay heavily for your failure."

Kaga looked at Sandy who gave him a short nod.

"No, no, leave her alone. I'll let you enter."

"Hakana, they are entering the cave now."

"That's ok. You have to soar up into the air and through the clouds as soon as they walked in. We are right underneath you."

Kaga stood in front of Charc and Benishoson, he stretched out his arm, touched a spot outside the cave and then disappeared inside without getting tortured. The two red dragons were able to follow him unimpaired. The passage descended into the depths of the mountain. A mysterious purple light illuminated their way which merged into a matt light-orange at the end. Kaga rushed faster and faster down the trail. He almost blended into the rock face and suddenly he was gone.

"The bastard has fooled us!" Charc cursed furiously.

"No son, have a look! All these thousands of protective stones are ours. We only have to pick them."

Benishoson didn't care whether Kaga managed to escape or not. He pondered frantically how he could get rid of his son in order to gain sole possession of these stones."

Suddenly he heard a voice.
"Benishoson, Descendant of Benisho, The Shining Light. This is Ikechi, Adama's Power. Get out of there and face the battle! Face me!"
"That can't be true!"
His head was spinning. His allies had told him that Ikechi was eliminated.

"You wait here inside the cave until I have taken care of Ikechi."
Benishoson didn't even wait for an answer but dashed out of the cave. Ikechi blocked his way, facing the rising sun. He was willing to put up with this disadvantage as he wanted to make full use of the sun when applying his gem.
Benishoson laughed coldly,
"Haven't we already experienced a similar situation before?! But this time the result will be different."
"What makes you so sure about that?"
"I know that you are hurt. And I'll take advantage of that."

Ikechi shot a stream of fire at Benishoson who immediately sent a stream back. But they didn't cause any harm, they just fizzled out. Adama's Power was highly concentrating on his stone. He bundled the sun light and released it from the center of his gold nugget, directing it at his opponent. But unfortunately to no avail as Benishoson had seen the beam coming. In a flash, he turned his head and body away. Ikechi then tried to target at Benishoson's central stone at close range. He grabbed The Descendant of Benisho with his mighty front claws, clutched his enemy's tail tightly with his own and at the same time pushed with his snout his foe's snout down towards the ground. Ikechi wanted to destroy Benishoson's crucial gemstone with a single strike. Benishoson winced,

"You are supposed to be dead or at least seriously injured. What has gone wrong?"

Ikechi noticed these words only subconsciously but they triggered his thoughts.

"From where does he know that I was injured? What had he got to do with it?"

But then he focused his mind only on his fight. Benishoson realized that he wasn't able to handle Ikechi who had obviously recovered from his injury he had suffered. He gathered all this strength and pulled away from his opponent, then tried to find a way out.

Charc didn't intend to obey his father's orders. He immediately turned to the stones.

"Which one shall I take first?"

He eagerly scanned the walls. A round jewel, gleaming yellow, attracted his attention at once. He used his beam to cut it out of the rock. It needed his full concentration. He had done this before when he had burnt out the bloodstones. So why shouldn't it work again here inside the cave? He drilled his beam accurately between stone and rock.

"What's that?"

The Red stared in great astonishment at the result. A thick red liquid trickled down the rock face. After a short moment it solidified and its color turned back into yellow.

"Protective stones are not soft. They are tough and can withstand the heat of my beam."

He repeated the procedure three-times but it always led to the same result.

"Do gems become so soft and useless during the course of time?"

He tried picking up a piece. But when grabbing it, it shattered into thousand pieces. He couldn't force back his impatience any longer. With his right claw he hit furiously against the rock, splintering it to pieces. His mighty tail crashed against the wall. And again, the stones he had hit burst into pieces. The more he disturbed the more he quivered all over with rage. Grimly he burned one section after another until he was surrounded by a ring of fire. His outburst had a disastrous effect. The stones he had struck flowed down the wall looking like tears.

"Was that a curse? Were the gemstones protected by a special spell?"

The Red didn't know what to do when he suddenly heard the hated voice of his half-brother calling him,

"Charc, get out of there and fight. It's time to account for your actions."

"What is Draco doing here? And where is Benishoson?"

Well, Draco wouldn't be a challenge for him.

THE FAVORED FEW

Ikechi chased Benishoson mercilessly across The Invisible Summits while an intense battle raged on in the Cave of the Sparkling Stones. Rocket had informed Hakana about the cave's precise location whereupon Hakana had given this information to Sandy. She was genuinely worried about losing all the stones in case their immaculacy planned strategy would fail. Kaga was supposed to guard the entrance. But would he also be able to manage handling Charc and Benishoson? As soon as The Reds had disappeared inside the cave Sandy immediately sent a message to The Favored Few and then joined them. Instantaneously they arranged their battle array. Ikechi was the first to challenge Benishoson. While he was confident about his victory, the others put their rehearsed plan into practice. It was Draco who began with his part.

"Charc, get out of there and fight. It's time to account for your actions."

Charc lashed his tail again, and thereby burst many more stones before leaving the cave. Full of confidence he planted himself in front of Draco. They were facing one another.

"Well my dear brother, how are you going to defeat me without breaking the codex? I have no scruples about putting an end to your life."

Draco's emerald glinted brightly and his entire body turned a shade darker.

"I am well aware of that. But there are different possibilities."

A sudden beam coming from Draco's stone took The Red by surprise. Still during the process of firing, Draco disappeared behind Charc. Charc was puzzled.

"Where are you? Don't hide like a frightened rabbit. Fight like a dragon!"

"That's what we are doing."

Instead of Draco Rocket was facing The Red now. He lowered his head and cocked his dark beard up to its full height. His fellow combatants did exactly the same. Draco was hoovering on the opposite side of Rocket. He was glowing dark-green. The Red hadn't even noticed that Hakana and Diane had placed themselves on either side of Draco. Sandy and Nero were staying a bit further away.

"Do they believe to defeat me with their battle array? They'll have to do better than that if they want to destroy me."

It only caused Charc to sneer.

"I'll wipe them out with a single stroke of my tail if they try to attack me from behind."

But then Rocket's protective stone started to blaze which startled Charc slightly.

"What are you up to now, you bastard? Are you sure you can cope with me? Not even your father had the courage to do so."

Suddenly all of his enemy's stones gleamed in their own color.

But not a single jet of fire was targeted at The Red but instead light flashes illuminated the surroundings. All of them were emitted towards Rocket which he then bundled with the help of his gemstone.

Charc's smile was triumphant.

"Sure, why don't they kill themselves if they are stupid enough to do so? I've no objections."

Charc was just about to release a massive jet of fire towards Rocket when he felt as if he had been struck by lightning. Something had hit his stone. He shook himself. Rocket had used his protective stone to bundle and reinforce the collected light with his own light. He then had aimed at The Red's black diamond. Before he was even able to respond, a second stream of light beams followed. The black inclusions in Charc's stone were highly conductive carbon particles which turned his white diamond black. His alleged strength became his weakness. Draco, Hakana and Diane delivered supply so that Rocket could maintain an uninterrupted barrage at Charc's star which eventually caused it to glow. Rocket didn't stop the barrage until Charc's star exploded into a thousand pieces. Too many beams of light had circled inside his stone until it couldn't hold these any longer and made it burst. Diamond slivers flew around in every direction. Charc felt how his movements became labored. Fatigue drained him of strength. He had only his bloodstones left. But these were worthless without his star. All these little young dragons had to die for nothing. A last jet of light destroyed the rest of his gem. The Red was defeated. He had turned into a run-down copy of his Pink Brigade just like any other of its members. His bright color faded into a pale pink. He wasn't any different from any other member. Run-down and weak.

He refused to believe that.

"I will come back and then I will kill you all!"

"Daddy, don't let him escape!"

Sandy barred his way.

"May I just take your bloodstones? They aren't yours. They have never belonged to you. We'll give them a dignified farewell in the eternal fire."

The Red was robbed of all his power. From now on he had to spend his life as a pink outcast. Even worse he would spend the rest of his life without a protective stone.

The Favored Few, Sparkle and Silent Wings felt an overwhelming joy about their victory. For the dragons' world all danger was past. But the rage and the despair that Charc had ruined the Cave of the Sparkling Stones outweighed their delight. Then Nero explained his fellows.

"I was absolutely convinced that the gems of the deceased dragons are kept in the Cave of the Sparkling Stones."

 "Well, they are."

"But these aren't gemstones. They glitter and glisten but they aren't gemstones."

"You are right."

"But what are they?"

"When I was on my way to The Ten Thousand Islands of the Rising Sun, I noticed a small isle. It blazed in the most dazzling of colors. When I perched there the gemstones cracked under my weight. Until today I haven't found out what they are. But they are a marvelous substitute."

"Are you saying that this isn't the Cave of the Sparkling Stones?"

"Exactly! I had racked my brain how we could get Charc into the cave without raising suspicion. Then I remembered seeing these stones on that very island. I asked Rocket to fly to Kaga and to inform him about my plan. Kaga should find another cave and attach these stones at its walls. Kaga was supposed to trick Charc into the cave by pretending this was the Cave of the Sparkling Stones. The Chronicler agreed and with Rocket's help they finished just in time. He installed additional protective measures to make it even more difficult for Charc to enter. Here you can see the result. The cave has truly been damaged but it had served its purpose."

"That is brilliant!"

"I hadn't talked to anybody about this apart from Rocket and Kaga. Your outrage about the sanctuary's destruction should have looked real."

"Well, that obviously worked out very well."

IKECHI

Ikechi did everything to keep his promise which he had given to Hinto. Benishoson's expulsion from Muraco. He would fight for that with all his heart.

He pursued Benishoson across the white peaks towards the east and realized that The Ten Thousand Islands of the Rising Sun were his destination. The Descendant of Benisho dived into a flat band of clouds which obscured Ikechi's vision. And then he had suddenly vanished.

"That's just not possible!"

Ikechi strained his wings and climbed higher into the sky to get a better view. Nothing.

"He is gone without a trace."

A maelstrom down in the water caught his attention. Had he dived into it? Adama's Power spiraled down, angled into a shallow dive and slowly approached the surface where he scanned the water with a searching gaze. Nothing. But suddenly a silver-shining arrow shot out of the ocean. He rammed his sharp rotated horn right into his belly and turned it 360 degrees to make it worse, pulled it out and disappeared into the depth of the sea. Ikechi already knew this burst of agony. These horns had inflicted a grievous wound once before in his belly. He could feel that he was profusely bleeding.

"Hopefully, I will be strong enough to get to Chendris."

With his last ounce of strength, he reached the peninsula. Stella had given him some of Rubi's water which he drippled into the wound. Then he blacked out.

When consciousness finally came back, he had a strong feeling of deja vu. Sparkle was crouching next to him, glancing at him with his big blue worried eyes. But something was different this time. At his left side there was a black dragon with an orange belly who also looked rather concerned. It was his grand-son Nero. And in front of him there was Silent Wings, his grand-daughter. They had followed him immediately after they had defeated The Red. But they hadn't expected to find him in such a terrible state. Even though he was seriously injured he was still having a clear mind. Had it been pure coincidence or had he been neatly trapped? Then he fell into a bleary trance again.

Ikechi could sense that his time was coming to an end. He begged his grandkids to accompany him to the Cave of the Sparkling Stones.

Nero sadly pointed out,

"Grandpa, we don't even know where the cave is."

"Don't worry. As I am about to die, we will be guided. Kaga is also going to help you."

The three siblings helped Ikechi flying. Silent Wings took the lead. The injured dragon put his head and his body on her back. Nero and Sparkle supported his wings. One on each side. Their outline formed a large triangle in the sky. They flew underneath the clouds close to the vegetation line. The mountains underneath them were covered by evergreen trees. Above them steep peaks rose up to the sky which were interspersed with scattered clouds. They were taken by surprise when Kaga suddenly blocked their way.

"I've heard that the mighty Ikechi is ready to die. Follow me!"

Kaga twisted up into the clouds. The three dragons did as instructed, carrying

Adama's Power with them. Shortly after they landed on a platform.

"Thank you, my precious kids. But from here I've to go on my own."

Kaga was the first to enter the cave. Ikechi followed him laboriously. But turned around once more.

"Sparkle, please wait here. I have one last wish."

Then he vanished into the den.

It didn't take long and Kaga returned.

"Ikechi, Adama's Power, has given away his protective stone. Sparkle, please accompany me inside. His legacy to you is to share his knowledge."

Sparkle followed Kaga into the cave. Never before in his life had he seen something so gorgeous and sparkly. The stones which were embedded into the wall were glittering and twinkling.

"Come on Sparkle. Here is Ikechis's stone. Are you prepared to accept Ikechi's legacy?"

Sparkle answered simply and seriously,

"Yes, I am."

"Then go ahead and touch Ikechi's gem with your own stone. This will transfer his entire knowledge onto you which will enable you to fulfill his legacy more easily."

346

Sparkle did as instructed. Both stones lit up brightly. Ikechi's last thought emerged in Sparkle's subconsciousness.

"As a young dragon the world belongs to you. And the time which we have at our disposal seems endless. But suddenly one day, we notice that our time is finite but our unfinished tasks don't become less. We can't continue indefinitely. And therefore I'd like to leave you my legacy."

From now on Sparkle knew about the battles Ikechi had fought, which doubts he had had and which secrets he had harbored. Sparkle felt proud that he had received these new tasks. And with that Sparkle had changed.

FIRE CEREMONY

Kaga had prepared Ikechi for his last voyage. Three strong lianas were tied around his body; two around his wings and one around his tail. As the male family members were present, who had the task to escort the dead body, Ikechi was promptly transported into the direction of The Ten Thousand Islands of the Rising Sun. Draco, as his son, had the honor to guard the right flank. Sparkle, possessing the legacy of Adama's Power, guarded his left flank. Nero supported his tail while Rocket was the rearguard. This flight was an extraordinary event for Sparkle. It was the first time that he experienced Muraco, The World of The White Moon, with his own eyes and at the same time perceived the events from Ikechi's perspective. He saw the wild chase after Benishoson, his sudden disappearance in the clouds, the desperate search for his old enemy, the emergence of the maelstrom which was still in turmoil underneath them. And he could also perceive the silver flash and the agonizing pain which he had already experienced earlier on in his life.

"Sparkle, what's the matter?"
Since Sparkle had been lost in his mental pictures, he hadn't noticed that he had slowed down.
"Nothing."
All of them payed full attention again on their task carrying the important freight towards the east to The Ten Thousand Islands of the Rising Sun. When they arrived at the foot of Ahote-Hakan, The Restless Fire, they put their valuable good down. They would rest by its side for one sunset. In the light of the following rising sun they would hand him over to the volcano. During this process they were chanting sad songs describing Ikechi's final journey.

"Descendant of Erwaen and Berhane
Brother of Adama, The Oracle
That was Ikechi, Adama's Power

Fought bravely
for many hundred rotations

A last time
cowardly ambushed

The beast is waiting
for its penalty

Bold Ikechi
at sunrise you will be handed over to
Ahote-Hakan,
The Restless Fire,
so that you may go peacefully over to
your ancestors"

At sunrise the escort climbed up to the lip of the volcano. They could see the blazing red lava boiling underneath them. As if by a secret signal the lianas snapped off his body and released Ikechi, letting him glide into the fire. As a final tribute each dragon, including Rocket, shot an additional mighty beam of fire. Ikechi had returned to the ancestral land.

Sandy had given the bloodstones to Draco which used to belong to Bernadette's kids. They also should be handed over to Ahote-Hakan, to finally pay them their last respect. After the dignified funeral all four dragons soared above the endless ocean, heading east.

Their destination was the northern part of the mainland in order to rescue Bernadette.

Bernadette was quickly freed. For The Favored Few it was a very easy task to deal with the remaining members of the Pink Brigade. Without their boss they were a powerless bunch of dragons.

Bernadette collapsed in front of the diamond tomb of her kids. Big dragon-tears welled in her eyes and then flooded her face. The cruel fist which had clenched her heart for so many rotations eventually loosened. The iron ring burst into pieces. The nightmare was over. She wouldn't stay in this den any longer. A new future spread its magnificence out before her. Mightily relieved they headed towards the Assembly Place.

THE ASSEMBLY

While Draco, Sparkle, Nero and Rocket had been setting off east with Ikechi, Hakana, Sandy, Silent Wings and Diane made their farewell to Kaga. Their destination was the Council of the Seven Stones at the Assembly Place. They took off and turned westward. On their way they were telling everyone about the forthcoming extraordinary meeting. The news was spreading faster than the four could fly. And so, it came that traders already clustered the place when they arrived. The ones who loved to celebrate had already set up their camps. Dragons were coming from all directions. Everyone wanted to give a worthy farewell to Ikechi, Adama's Power. Hakana gave a rough overview to the Council of Benishoson's escape and Charc's disempowerment. She noticed, just as Ikechi had already noticed before, that Hinto's eyes, usually looking rather indifferent, lit up briefly when he heard about Ikechi's final journey into the Cave of the Sparkling Stones.

When Draco, Sparkle, Nero and Rocket also arrived a little later with Bernadette the cheering was immense. Stella was beside herself with joy when she finally saw her sister again. They had a lot to talk about. Sad aspects predominated their conversation.

As a final tribute to all of his heroic deeds they praised Ikechi while gathering around various fires. From sunset to sunrise they kept singing, laughing, eating, drinking and dancing.

It was a dignified gathering that guided Ikechi, Adama's Power, the way to his ancestors.

FAREWELL

After celebrating, the smooth passage of Ikechi's soul to his ancestors for thirty sunrises and sunsets, the dragons parted again. Draco had spent a few sunrises with Stella. Even though they had kept a bit off the beaten track he now longed for his cliff from where he could look out for a hurricane in order to perform his favorite occupation. Sparkle, Nero and Diane accompanied him to the north-east. In order to fulfill their destiny. Rocket shot himself into the orbit to explore space. Silent Wings and Rubi, who had also attended the celebration, continued their lives as wanderers in the service of the dragons on Muraco, The World of The White Moon. Hakana had obtained the permission to be taught by Kaga from The Council of the Seven Stones. Sandy would join her.

Stella approved Bernadette's idea to raise the hatchlings in her cave. Thus, they returned and Bernadette laid her eggs. After half a rotation four hatchlings finally flopped out of their shells. One was as orange as Stella, another one was reddish-brown taking after its mother. The next resembled its grandmother Raiffa and the last one was fiery red with a black comb, red eyes and black pupils.

Ressources:

Heilsteine, Julia Labacher
Die Farben der Arktis, A Greenpeace Book
Die Welt in der wir leben, Knaur Verlag
www.mineralienatlas.de
wikipedia.org/wiki/Ultraviolettstrahlung
www.vorname.com
www.pixabay.com
www.diamanten-diamant.de
www.pinterest.de
www.karrer-edelsteine.de

www.ingramcontent.com/pod-product-compliance
Lightning Source LLC
Chambersburg PA
CBHW030917050726
47498CB00003BA/789